NYM

The Se

'For me, at all even
way in life I simply l

NYMPH IN PARIS

Galia S.
Translated by Nicholas Courtin

A STAR BOOK
published by
the Paperback Division of
W. H. ALLEN & Co. PLC

A Star Book
Published in 1984
by the Paperback Division of
W. H. Allen & Co. PLC
44 Hill Street, London W1X 8LB

First published in France by
Éditions Robert Laffont, S.A., Paris, 1983
under the title *La Déchaîne*

Printed and bound in Great Britain by
Anchor Brendon Ltd, Tiptree, Essex

ISBN 0 352 31456 7

'You only get to heaven by overindulgence'
Twelfth century heretical saying

I
DISCOVERY

April 8, 1981

Anything can happen in Paris, but today was unprecedented.

Promptly at 11 a.m. Prince Jemal Abdelaziz El Faraoud came into view striding up Avenue George V with 40 camels in tow.

As arranged, Osvaldo and I were waiting at the corner *terrasse* of *Fouquet's* celebrated restaurant.

We sighted the animals afar off as they sauntered past an incredulous public with their noses in the air. His Excellency looked alert enough but you would think the camels had seen it all before.

To obtain a better view, Osvaldo and I clambered onto our chairs. We saw Prince Jemal approaching with the first camel, which was towing the second camel, and so on as far as No. 40. The royal camel-driver halted in front of us and tied the first camel to a lamp-post. He then advanced towards us, took my hand and brushed it with his lips, shook Osvaldo's, and beamed at us in triumph.

'My word is my bond. Here are the camels,' he declared
with his palms turned upwards.

Whereupon he spun round and walked briskly to his
Rolls-Royce or Bentley or whatever it was at the rear of No.
40, and rode off with a majestic purr.

Osvaldo was thunderstruck. Never had he imagined that
Jemal would actually keep his pledge. After all, we had all
been pretty inebriated that night. My Italian handed me
down from my chair, and glowered at the camels.

A week ago we had sat on the steps of the Pantheon:
Osvaldo, the Prince, myself and a redhead whose name
escapes me. In the chilly pre-dawn wind, Jemal had risen to
his feet and waved the bottle: 'I wish to propose a toast!'

We had come from a deafening smoke-filled nightclub,
Jemal had seized a magnum of champagne from a waiter
and, cramming a wad of banknotes into his pocket, had
commanded four glasses to be brought to the steps of the
illustrious Pantheon monument.

There, the swaying Prince turned to me and announced:
'To your eyes, Galia! To your eyes, which are the colour of
the Canadian lakes!'

'Canadian,' Osvaldo managed to respond. 'Quite so.'

'So that's it,' I rejoined. 'To my eyes!'

We downed our glasses in one go, and stared at the asphalt
desert before us. It was growing cold with the first light of
day.

'And now let us talk business,' said Jemal, grasping
Osvaldo by the arm. 'We shall return shortly, O beautiful
ladies.'

The two men went off, and the redhead threw herself into
my arms and wailed: 'He doesn't love me, he doesn't love
me.'

The Chanel No. 5 still clinging to her, the redhead
swamped my neck with tears and snuffled in my ear: 'Why
doesn't he love me?' I patted her on the back and consoled
her as best I could. She took my head in both hands, planting
a pulpy kiss on my lips. That was nothing to the surprise that

10

lay in wait for me.

The men came back, I delicately shoved the redhead into the princely arms, and drew a heavy-eyed Osvaldo to one side. I was worried about all this secrecy.

'Fixed up your deal?'

'Er, well yes, actually.'

'How's that actually? Bought an oil well?'

'As a matter of fact I have sold you to Jemal for 40 camels.'

'You did what!'

'He said to me "She is very beautiful is Galia" and I said "How true", he said "She's highly sexy", I said "absolutely, highly sexy", he said "I give you 10 camels for her", I said it wasn't enough and he bid 20 camels.'

The concept of twenty camels failed to impinge itself on my mind. I wondered how long a caravan of 20 camels would look.

Osvaldo continued: '"Thirty camels", well I still hesitated and he shouted "FORTY CAMELS!", so I said "Stop yelling, it's a deal, 40 camels".'

My Italian paused, and then told me: 'We shook hands to make it official and he said "You got yourself a contract, a week from now at 11 a.m. outside *Fouquet's* you hand over Galia and I give you the camels. Do not forget, April 8, 11 o'clock!"'

So there we were today at 11.30 a.m. with the camels. They were gazing across at the store windows in the Champs-Elysées as if they were in some Arab *souk*.

Osvaldo was none too pleased, I could tell. He has an in-built dislike of animals, even nice inoffensive ones like cats and dogs and birds. And there he was, the owner of 40 camels who, to make matters worse, were treating him with utter disdain. He began pacing up and down the pavement, scowling at these ships of the desert now berthed on one of the poshest street corners in the world.

People were starting to gather, asking the silliest questions: 'Is it for a film? Who's starring in it? Are they camels or dromedaries? Can we have a ride mister?'

Osvaldo was losing his cool: 'Filthy damn things. I'm not touching the beasts. Jemal can take them away again or I'll just leave – Ah, here he is again!'

The glorious Rolls or Bentley pulled into the curb, thus providing a further attraction for the crowd. The chauffeur, impeccably turned out in an ash-grey uniform and peaked cap, got out and opened the rear door to release his master. The Arabian magnate advanced straight at us, looked into my eyes and proffered a huge bouquet of roses.

Twisting my mouth, I murmured to Osvaldo: 'His word is his bond.'

'He can go and stuff his camels ...'

The smiling Jemal took me by the arm: 'My dear Osvaldo, I am enchanted with our little contract ...'

'Now listen, Prince, I think there's been some mis-understanding. After all, it was just a joke. April the First, you know? We always have jokes on April the First, ha ha!'

The other's eyes turned as black as a barrel of crude Arabian Heavy and he pinched my arm: 'I never treat women as a joke. Or contracts either. Come Galia.'

There was no longer any doubt, I had been exchanged for a bunch of camels and there was no going back. I was now the property of Prince Jemal Abdelaziz El Faraoud.

I am now penning these lines in my luxurious room at the Plaza Hotel, in a confused state of anxiety, curiosity and excitement. Apart from Osvaldo, I have known not man, as they say in the Bible. My Prince is out fixing up more deals, and has not laid a finger on me so far. He has been treating me royally and I want for nothing.

Tonight we are to celebrate, he says, just the two of us – alone!

With this new chapter of my life now opening up, I have resolved to keep a diary of everything that happens from now on.

I am trying to picture the expression on my father's face if he ever learns that his 20-year-old daughter has been sold for 40 camels. And what he would say if he could see her astride the bidet in this antiquated palace, soaping herself as she awaits her Prince of Araby for a night of love.

Poor old Daddy, working his fingers to the bone to give his children a decent, strict, catholic and patriotic education all those years.

He so badly wanted a son, two sons even, so that he could hand on the warrior's torch to posterity! Alas, the first child was a girl, and the second another. But he didn't give up and decided the next was bound to be his longed-for Hubert. But Huberte arrived in the feminine, and he had another go. Cecile let him down and after her it was me, Galia. Then he gave up!

Stuck with five daughters, he went ahead and grimly made a living as a stockbroker in the ancient city of Tours. As a result of his chagrin, Mummy is becoming more and more neurotic as the years go by. Daddy hasn't slept with her properly for simply ages, that's obvious. She must be frantic in our provincial town where all their friends are so straightlaced and an affair with an outsider unthinkable.

I know how agonizingly frustrated she must be. She runs a mobile library for the respectable citizens of Tours and its environs: Voltaire, Hugo, Diderot and the 'moderns' like Bazin, Sabatier, Bodard and Tournier. She also helps with the local festival and concerts and recitals. And to cheer her lonely evenings, she translates English poetry.

The fact is that my parents have nothing left to talk about. The five of us have left home, and they spend their evenings on the balcony at the old family house, contemplating the River Loire in silence, thinking their own thoughts, he with a glass of whisky in his hand, she sipping herb tea.

Silence. We were not talkers in our family. At least we discussed nothing of importance. Mealtimes were never occasions at which we really communicated. There was no fun to it at all, just remarks about school reports, a cousin who got engaged, a squeaky tap in the bathroom. Personally I would have liked to know some of the essential matters; for example, for months I wanted to know how boys got an erection. What caused it? I would think about this in bed at night. 'Perhaps they do it like the swimming coach when he shows off his biceps and the muscles stick out,' I would say to myself. 'They concentrate, make it happen by willpower and their thing goes stiff.'

I wondered if the penis was a muscle or perhaps a bone that advances and retracts afterwards. I longed to know, too, why my sisters had hair under their arms and between their legs, and what it was for. When I asked my mother in all innocence, she would look away: 'We'll discuss all that when you are a big girl.' She was quite snooty about it.

I would keep on: 'Please Mummy, when a man and a lady are married, how do they have babies? I don't understand about the seeds. Has the husband got seeds in his thing?'

I had seen little boys with no clothes on when we went to the beach, and I used to imagine their penises full of ground coffee or corn or rice and worry about how it came out.

It wasn't my fault. At the Ursuline Convent where I went to school, the sisters were no help at all. Sex was a forbidden word, and the subject was surrounded in mystery and terror. They knocked three things into us:

1. Sex is the work of the devil.
2. The less fun you have, the more merit you accumulate.
3. Beware of men.

Of course these rules were never actually spoken or put down in writing, but the sisters at the Collège Sainte-Ursule managed to say it in a sneaky sort of way.

So we had to hide what we did, conceal our moments of pleasure and cheat the 'cops in coifs', as we nicknamed them. One of these was dreadful, Sister Marie-Thérèse the geography teacher – her ruling passion was masturbation.

After class she would often get one of the girls to herself, and try to make her confess everything, wheedling it out of her.

'Clotilde, my dear, you seem rather pale these days, are you getting enough sleep?'

'Oh yes, Sister Marie-Thérèse.'

14

'Of course, but before you fall asleep, do you find your hand wandering?'

'Wandering, sister?'

'I mean do you caress yourself just a little bit?'

'Caress, Sister?'

'Yes, you know what I mean.'

And the girl would gaze at her trustingly with a sanctimonious daughter-of-Mary look. Some of my small friends were genuinely mystified, but Sister Marie-Thérèse with her hole-in-the-corner chats made sure they began their nocturnal explorations very soon afterwards.

I suppose I was rather advanced for my age, because I didn't need her advice. I learned how to do it all by myself, and most nights I would reach down for the tiny magic button so conveniently placed. Hardly needing to move, I could bring on the loveliest tingly feelings with nobody even knowing. Several of us did.

April 9, after midnight

It is certainly exotic, spending the night in a palatial room in Paris so close to my own studio-apartment.

At the moment Jemal is asleep in his room, which connects with mine through the bathroom.

A few hours ago he rather ceremoniously handed me a gift-wrapped box saying: 'This is for you Galia. Let us prepare ourselves.' Naturally I couldn't wait, and tore off the paper and lid to discover the most gorgeous white silk nightdress with spangles and trimmings straight out of a fairy tale.

I duly 'prepared' myself. First a hot bath using three perfume essences, then long and languid brushing of the hair, torrid make-up somewhat overdone by European standards, and then the alluring nightdress that might almost have been an evening dress for dinner downstairs. Underwear was not allowed, and as the silk material was semi-transparent the whole effect was most suggestive. I swayed my hips to see how I looked in motion.

A knock at the door, and I swallowed nervously. My bosom heaved as I sought to remain calm, and my throat released a mere squeak as I said: 'Come in.' I put my arms over my breasts modestly.

The door opened towards me, and there was His Excellency head high and dressed to kill, as it were, in a kind of de luxe thin wrap fringed with *lamé*.

We stood for a while facing each other. I dared not move and Jemal seemed almost as nervous.

At least to begin with. But I already saw that I came up to his expectations, for his shiny garment started to bulge just below his waist.

In a voice deep with emotion he declared: 'O Galia Galia, you are so truly beautiful.'

'So are you, truly,' I whispered.

'We could, could ...'

'Yes Jemal?'

'We could take a glass of champagne together. I will call room service ... Hullo, send up a Dom Perignon, the best year you have! Without delay!'

The strained wrap front divulged his rising impatience, and my own excitement increased. But he came no nearer, made no move to touch me, not even bestowing a first kiss. He remained distant, aloof – and erect. When the waiter came in, quietly efficient, pushing a small trolley into the room, Jemal made no attempt to conceal his protuberance. I was embarrassed. We watched as the man presented the bottle of '48 and slowly released the cork. Like a dancing priest, he poured two glasses and returned the bottle to the ice bucket, delicately placing some napkins on the tray.

By now we were seated in armchairs, some distance apart, observing the ceremonial wordlessly.

The waiter went on and on, and Jemal suddenly rose, dismissing the man without more ado.

'That is enough,' he ordered. 'I will see to the rest. You go now!'

16

The waiter, paid to do as he was told and submit to a hundred small humiliations daily, left instantly and with practised dignity, closing the door soundlessly.

'Galia my beauteous one, let us drink to our love.'

We took our glasses, they went 'tink' as they met, and when I lowered my face to drink I saw his member lengthening visibly under the wrap. He seemed enormous.

I choked as he suddenly threw his glass across the room. He grabbed me by the arms, pulled me over to the bed and pushed me across it on my back. In a flash he lifted the skirt of my nightie, forced my legs apart, and violently penetrated me.

It was all over in three minutes.

Fighting to regain my breath I told him: 'My word, Jemal, you're not at all the sensual type.'

'Oh yes, Galia, I am. It was so good!'

I am now writing this in the still of the night. As politely as I could, I asked to sleep alone.

He had jumped me like a buck rabbit and it still hurts. How is it possible for a man to make love with so little know-how, so brutally and with so little tact? I do know that in the country it is an accepted thing in many homes for the womenfolk to be 'taken' silently in the dark, stealthily almost, with hardly a kiss. The male covers the female without preliminaries, jabs his implement in like she is some old sow, and gives a grunt. He shoots his semen and they turn their backs on each other, just as her juices are starting to flow. It's not fair, and in cotton nightclothes too!

How lucky I was to meet Osvaldo, to have been initiated by an experienced and sensitive pleasure-seeker, an understanding lover who knows how to woo, win and gratify a girl!

I was just 18 when he deflowered me, highly-principled and prim though I was. I was so terrified really. With my strict upbringing I had striven unyielding against the delights of sexual fulfilment, the ultimate forbidden fruit.

I would titter inwardly when I caught sight of a boy and

girl kissing and cuddling in public. How ridiculous they seemed to me, shrouded as I was in my own immaturity.

I am infinitely grateful to my first lover for patiently vanquishing my reserve, for piercing the heavy armour of my puritan morality.

It was simply marvellous the way it happened the first time. We had been playing tennis all morning on that hot July day at the Rueil-Malmaison Club. The score was 6-1, 6-2, 5-1, to Osvaldo. He is a far better player than I am but he lets me have a few points without me noticing it too obviously.

It was deuce, Osvaldo's service. His first serve went crashing into the net, the second overshot by a couple of yards. He served again from my right, an easy ball and not too fast. I whipped it neatly over to his corner, my point, 5-2, change ends. We sat down for a minute on a bench to wipe off our rackets and take a breather.

'You could have retrieved that, you must be getting past it,' I quipped, trying to control my breathing.

'Sorry, not a chance, I was off-balance. That was a fantastic back-hand.'

'And that second serve, miles out.'

'It happens to us all. My goodness, you're soaked, let me help you.'

He stood over me with the thick towel, patting my face, gently wiping my neck and arms and legs. I let him pamper me and closed my eyes. His mouth covered my open lips and I felt his tongue come inside, so slippery and naturally. Mmmm, it was nice. I had always kept my lips closed when a boy kissed me, but he caught me off-guard.

Exhausted and with the midday sun beating down, I melted.

He went on wiping me and it became a caress. He let the towel drop away and ran his hand over my shoulders, fingering my lips, my ears, and then my breasts so that my nipples became hard. He reached round my waist and in front and I instinctively clenched my thighs.

18

'Don't do that,' he murmured.

'Why?'

Was this the language of desire? I wondered. The 'Why?' had escaped, trickled out of its own volition. Was I asking him 'Why there?' or was I asking myself 'Why should I still resist my natural inclinations, why keep my thighs held tightly?'

Taking advantage of my confusion he moved his hand under my short pleated skirt and into my panties, swiftly pressing his fingers into my sex, now swollen and wet with perspiration.

I caught my breath but made no resistance as the first quiver jolted me. Osvaldo stroked me inside, back and forth, and I willed myself to concentrate on the little waves of pleasure spreading all over my pelvis. He changed to a lifting motion under my bottom, and I wanted him to go faster. My interior was pulsing when he gently halted and laid me on the bench, removing my panties. My thighs fell apart and I jerked several times when he resumed his caresses, the warm sun heightening my appetite.

Then a release of exquisite pleasure-pain seared through me, and I remember my head lashing from side to side. Never could I have imagined such volcanic rapture. Often by myself I had orgasms that left me shaking convulsively, but this was a scorching sirocco of joy.

My darling Osvaldo helped me to the changing room. There was nobody else there and he spread our towels on the long seat. Minutes later he pierced my membrane, causing me to cry out in a near coma.

When I recovered, a glow of triumph enveloped my whole body and soul. I have never looked back, for on that day on July I exorcised the ghosts of the past once and for all.

One of the most evil aspects of the pathological tradition in which I was raised – they call it 'civilization' – is the fierce, dark determination of those who govern and educate us to prevent other people having enjoyment at all costs.

In some countries they cut the clitoris of growing girls, and in others they give them a missal. What is the difference? The significance is the same: women may not have fun, women are not made to gratify their senses.

Clitoridectomy and the catechism have kept women in chains for long centuries.

April 10

Today the Prince took me shopping in the Faubourg Saint-Honoré. We went by taxi around mid-morning, and when it came to settling the fare, Jemal said he carried no small change. He thereupon handed the driver 500 francs and waved his hand. I exchanged wide-eyed looks with the man behind the wheel.

We toured the boutiques, and he asked to see the best of everything. But he never questioned the price.

I must admit that this display of endless wealth made me quite heady; we didn't have oil wells at Tours. Money for Jemal was just continuous stationery, enabling him to satisfy his slightest whim – including me, of course! As Jemal approached, doors opened miraculously, broad smiles appeared, all kinds of people bowed low. His hand plunged again and again into an inexhaustible supply of paper money. I felt like the Queen of Sheba.

We visited a fine art gallery where he acquired a priceless jade statuette. As we left, I could restrain myself no longer. I was dying to knew where the money really came from. It was a tricky moment.

'Jemal,' I said as sweetly as Turkish delight, 'how nice for you not to run short of cash, ever.'

He got the message: 'I work for my living.'

'Yes?'

'I buy, I sell, I buy, I sell. Very simple.'

'How interesting,' I said breathlessly. 'But what?'

'Anything there is: oil, land, apartments, companies – anything.'

'It's nice being very rich, you must be very satisfied.'

'Oh no. The more I have the more I want. I work very hard, I am never satisfied.'

'I see, it's a kind of game.'

'Yes, I play with money. Only the rich can afford to play, only the rich get richer.'

'How exciting.' I ventured to add: 'Are you glad you bought me?'

'Oh Galia! I did not buy you. You are my guest!'

'Was I worth 40 camels?' My voice would have melted granite.

'My dear Galia, I would have offered a hundred camels for you!'

'I – a hundred camels! Oh Jemal, that's the nicest thing any man has ever said to me!'

April 11

I have always been starved of affection. It is my father's fault, he is such a hard man.

I have never been drawn to him, largely because he shows no warmth or tenderness towards Mummy. I shall never forgive him for withholding the love she deserves. He has wrecked a wonderful woman's entire existence.

Mummy had so many qualities: beauty, intelligence, a deep feeling for music and poetry, boundless generosity. She devoted herself unstintingly to us and to this man, who failed to show her understanding of any kind, cared nothing for her as a person. Naturally she became docile and arid. My father has to answer for such waste. Like many men of his generation, and indeed of today's, he thinks he owns her, body and soul. She is there to serve him, to be available at all times.

After five children and a miscarriage, she was dried out and the years started to tell. Father went with other women, and she became old in a matter of months.

April 12

I feel so guilty about missing my Thai language course and even more my dancing lessons which I love. I am sure I shall regret this later.

Too bad, I am in this up to my neck. The telephone is permanently switched to the answering machine and I am just letting myself drift. My Prince is my auto-pilot.

I simply let him decide everything, as long as he keeps on adoring me and treats me right. What else could a girl ask for amid the bright lights of Paris?

It was the *baccalaureat* that earned me Paris. Daddy promised to send me if I passed, and the glittering prospect was irresistible for a young girl pining away in the provinces.

During the final year I worked morning, noon and night cooped up like a nun. And when I passed with a distinction my father could not refuse. I knew he hated letting me off the leash, but a promise is a promise.

When I got off the train and walked to the exit, I felt like Balzac's Rastignac in skirts, or rather jeans as it happened. Alone and free outside the Gare D'Austerlitz, my heart leapt. No more grim-faced sisters in their silly coifs with their dreary prattling, no more dismal boring hours and hours at home. I was in Paris, Queen of all the cities. My mood was euphoric.

April 13

Prince Jemal has had me for three days and nights. It has been a gloriously hectic round of nightclubs, five-star restaurants and fabulous presents. Not forgetting the superb Plaza Hotel that would turn any girl's head.

But I am restless somehow. He is nice, attentive and generous, but the sexual side is disappointing. He makes love frantically, like a goat that's been locked up for weeks. We have no communication, he treats me as his property, his prize, to use how he wants.

It was fun at first but we are playing different games, and I feel the need for something different.

After breakfast today, Jemal took my hand and made me stand in front of him. He looked at me with his marvellous brown eyes.

'Galia, you are worried.'

'Oh no,' I said quietly.

'I know! There is an excellent restaurant at Rambouillet ...'

'Please Jemal, we have been to so many.'

'Galia, my adorable angel, you are making me suffer. What would you like more than anything else?'

'I would like to see the sea,' I whispered.

Within an hour the Rolls (I know now) was rushing us to Roissy Airport. A small private jet awaited us, the pilot standing to attention and a hostess with a creamy smile leading us out. We were off to Cannes, via Nice Airport.

April 15, 4 p.m., on a yacht

Cannes or Paris, it's all the same as they say in Montmartre. If you are with someone who is tiresome.

The Carlton Hotel took over from the Plaza and the restaurants are just as luxurious and sinister. To please me, Jemal has rented a sort of yacht with powerful engines and with all kinds of fancy equipment for deep sea fishing. We go to and fro on the azure blue of the Baie de Cannes, and then Jemal decides to let the engines go full out. We roar off out to sea like a torpedo.

At this speed you really have to hold on for dear life. The boat keeps crashing down on the waves and it is so noisy we can't hear ourselves shout.

I wave my arms like a mad thing, and Jemal slows down. Then he orders the engines to be stopped completely.

Ah, what peace, what bliss! Not a cloud in the sky as the boat rises and falls with the wavelets coming in from the horizon.

23

We lie down on the deck, rocking gently between sky and sea.

I can feel an immense warmth on my legs and abdomen. I have an urge to make love, to be in the arms of an experienced male.

It is a matter of seconds to remove the top of my two-piece bathing suit and the relief is immediate.

'Oh no,' orders Jemal. 'Please Galia, we are not alone!'

The captain, a young man with hair the colour of corn, smiles imperceptibly. He understands. Annoyed, I obey my Islamic lord and master, replacing my bra. It is noon and so sweaty.

'Shall we go for a swim?' I could not avoid the brittle tone.

'As you wish, Galia, your wish is my command' (Like hell!)

Me sultrily: 'Perhaps the captain, who hasn't told me his name, would like to bathe with us.' I hope I have clicked with him.

'With pleasure, Madame, very kind of you. I'd like to. My name is Yves.'

Jemal lowered the portcullis with a crash: 'You are being paid for your services as a captain. You will stay on board.'

So that was that, a swim in a chastity belt, and ordered with such lack of style. It may suit the Prophet but it's not my ethic, especially at 20 years of age. They can keep their yashmaks and their harems, they're not spoiling my fun just as it's starting to get interesting. I resolve to leave for Paris that very night, thumbing it all the way if I have to.

Later I put in a call to Mummy, suddenly feeling tender towards her. I nearly cried when she answered in her thin voice.

'Hullo.'

'Hullo Mummy, it's me.'

'My little pet!'

'Mummy I – I love you so very much. I just wanted to tell you right away.'

24

I heard her sob, and jammed down the receiver, biting my lip.

Ah, how I would love to be swept away like that for a man!

When I was a little girl I used to like a big cuddle on Mummy's lap after the evening meal. I can still smell her perfume, feel the wisps of hair tickling my cheek, her warm belly. We were united in a tranquil flow of love, our two bodies.

She used to recite her English poems to me, and I would half doze with my eyelids heavy as she translated the lines into French. That is how I started English, which is almost a second mother tongue for me.

I especially liked Milton. She would think a bit, recall a passage and recite it faultlessly in one go, calmly and softly. Once, the whole of *Lycidas*.

But it was heaven to me.

April 16, Montelimar, by the roadside

I can't get over it. I am 20, and I challenge anyone to deny that this is the most wonderful age for a girl.

At moments I want to hug myself, and frankly I'm worth hugging. I have a clear mind, good eyes, supple skin, I get hungry and thirsty, I love men, I love love, I love life!

Spring is a lovely season, full and radiant, and I am sitting on a lump of rock with a large piece of cardboard reading PARIS.

Trees are in blossom all around me, and for once even the motorway looks pretty.

I hardly slept last night but I am not tired.

Immediately we returned to harbour in Cannes, I knew what I had to do. I could not stay a minute longer with that lousy oil millionaire. I carefully wrapped all the presents he had bestowed on me over the past week and put them in a large suitcase. My personal things, not amounting to much, I stuffed in a beach bag.

I was all ready to go in my jeans and sailor jersey, with my

25

beach bag over my shoulder.

'Come Galia, we shall change for dinner, I have a surprise for you.'

'And so have I, a surprise for you.'

'For me, angel, what would that be?'

'This!!' And I hurled the case at the khaki-faced sheikh.

I did not have to wait long for transport. I thumbed a lift on La Croisette, the main promenade. A breakdown truck stopped, it could not have been more appropriate!

'Where to, Miss?' the truck driver enquired in his lilting *accent du Midi*.

'Anywhere.'

'Anywhere, just like that?'

'Anywhere, that's how it is.'

'Good, up you get.'

We had not gone 300 yards when he pulled up, and clamped his big mouth to mine. I let him have his thrill, and I rather liked it too.

We drew apart, panting like a pair of pigs. He wasn't bad looking and I fell for his local brogue.

'I'm a married man,' he said at length, 'but I've got life in me yet.'

'May I ask you something, please?'

'Go ahead, Miss.'

'Please take me to the motorway feeder, it's not far is it?'

'No, pretty near.' His rough hand was creeping over my knee and I froze. 'Maybe we could find a quiet spot ...' He eyed me lasciviously.

'I'm sorry, you're a real tonic, but I'm in a hurry to get to Paris. Please drive on, just take me to the motorway.'

The breakdown man had other ideas. He flashed a paw to my nodal point, but luckily my jeans are tough and he had trouble. Breathing hotly, he tried to force the zip. Even with both hands I could not push his fist away.

'Listen, please don't spoil it. Please! You were really decent just now, and now you can't control it, and I think you're being silly. It needs two to make love, or it's rape!'

26

No holding him off. He was getting nasty and kept on trying. The zip was undone and with a supreme effort I forced his fingers back and his hand came away. I broke free and jumped out.

As I stumbled away I could hear him yelling: 'Bloody whore. You're all the same, fucking cock-teasers ...'

I started thumbing again. An oldish man with greying hair took me as far as the motorway. He tried nothing, the perfect gentleman.

Getting lifts is certainly an eye-opener. It teaches you more about people than any textbook.

Next, a call to Osvaldo. He wasn't bitchy, thank goodness. Knew my voice right away and said 'Ah.' This, I assume, means 1) So you've turned up. 2) Are you alright? 3) I've got news.

'Anything you'd like to tell me?' I say, husky with sex-appeal.

'They've accepted my screenplay.'

'Fantastic! We've just got to celebrate that. I'm on my way back.'

'Where are you now?'

'In a motorist's paradise. I can see pink acrylic carseat covers, plastic dogs and cats for dangling in rear windows, cans marked "Regional Dish – Société Renard, Clichy", a line of ...'

'Where in God's name ...'

'I'm at a filling station on the *Autoroute du Sud,* see you soon. Oh I forgot, how are the camels?'

'I gave them away.'

'Who's the lucky fellow?'

'Chap in films. He was doing a low budget B picture about the Pharaohs with plywood palm-trees and everything. Now he's changed it to an adventure spectactular with real camels. He's got camels roaming all over the goddam studio. It's called Desert Caravan or Parched Desert or something like that ...'

Now, cars are hurtling by on the motorway like they are

27

afraid to run out of petrol. I may have picked a bad spot, in line with the sun. It was so easy yesterday, took only a minute for a lift to Montelimar.

It is a relief to be on your own in a small town you have never seen. You are not pressed for time and can do what you feel like.

But you have to keep alert. I went into a bistro packed with men and not a female in sight. I could almost hear them all sniffing at me. It was 10 p.m. and I was unaccompanied. Whatever they were thinking, all I wanted was a coffee.

I sipped it, mulling over the past week. I thought of the camels, and Jemal's face when I threw the suitcase at him, I am not a runaway person by nature, and this little escapade with a stranger, an Arab into the bargain, had its plus points too, I was thinking.

It could be that I am acquiring a taste for freedom. I'm not sure.

(Finish later. Car stopped and coming back to pick me up.)

April 21, Paris

Osvaldo obviously felt I was ripe for a new experience. Otherwise he would never dared to have taken me to *Le Bassano*, a highly private club off the Champs-Elysées protected by a thick oak door with copper reinforcements and a spyhole so that they can keep out the trash.

Within seconds, they whisked us inside, so Osvaldo is certainly a *habitué*. The manager shook hands and led us to the bar, an oldish man in a white silk shirt spread wide to display his hair-strewn tan who inspected me with the creased eyes of the experienced seducer and/or drinker.

I wriggled my bottom onto a bar stool *á la Hollywood* and tried to look *blasé*, registering the scene.

Diffused lighting, black and red lacquer walls, mirrors everywhere – awfully sophisticated. Leading off the end of the bar, a room with the door ajar.

That's when I did my first double-take.

A nude woman flitted by the doorway! At first I could not believe it. All I actually saw was a white shoulder, a mass of loose hair and a pair of heavyish buttocks. But there was no mistaking the fact: a grown woman with no clothes on had run past the opening.

My Italian mentor and the boss showed no sign of noticing. They were arguing about nudist club legislation on the Côte d'Azur, or pretending to.

Anyhow I gulped down some 12-year-old Ballantine to save face. Whisky always tastes like crushed bedbug to me, but at key moments like these it certainly keeps you on your stool.

My insides tingled as I sensed a whole new world through that doorway. A discreet orange light from within fuelled my interest, and I was so enervated I could not help fidgeting.

More bedbug in my glass, the clunk of an icecube, and Osvaldo drew near.

'Alright, my sweet?'

'Oh yes,' I squeaked. 'Just fine, handsome.'

'You look pale, treasure.'

'I feel absolutely divine.'

'You are adorable in that dress ...' I felt adorable, but I was nervous about it.

Osvaldo simply oozes romance. His voice was the thing that first appealed to me, of course. So musical! A sort of blend of Rossini, Puccini and Verdi: irony, melancholy and drama in a package deal. When it comes to charm you can't beat the Italians, I say.

Suddenly, there she was again! This time I heard the woman laugh, too. Rather dumpy she was, and I plainly saw the swell of her rump, her chestnut hair, her well-fleshed calves.

Behind a bland exterior, I was devoured with curiosity, longing to find out what they were doing in there. Osvaldo inched closer, smiled and offered his hand.

'Come, *tesoro,* I will take you in.'

I tumbled off my perch, slipped my hand in his and was

29

led, heart thumping, into the Holy of Holies.

What I saw there was quite devastating! I shall never forget it.

We were in a large room bathed in this dim orange light, and with a round bed in the middle 10 feet across. Couches heaped with sumptuous cushions lined the walls and on some of them men and women were lounging, most of them naked or almost, though a few still had their clothes on.

People were literally mawling one another. Couples and small groups writhed soundlessly except for the labour of heavy breathing. Then a woman started whispering hoarsely 'Oh, yes, there, there.' Someone was moaning, and I distinctly heard the gurgle of coital juices.

My eyes fixed on a stunning blonde in black satin wide knickers, suspender belt and the sheerest stockings. Her bra was off and I gazed upon two of the shapeliest golden boobies you could imagine; they were swelling and retracting prettily as she slowly caressed a phallus jutting from an open trouser zip. Except for his jacket the man was fully dressed and I was startled to see he still had his tie on.

His woman companion was too engrossed to notice us, and I continued looking at her bosom with a certain envy. Then on an impulse she bent down and her hair cascaded forward as she delicately enveloped the erect member with her lips. I was transfixed.

I pulled myself together and looked about to see a seated couple kissing hungrily, he fully dressed, she in the nude. She had her legs competely open and between them was a second woman on all fours licking and sucking at her cleft in generous motions. She too was naked and she arched her back so that her bottom assumed immense proportions. A rather mean-looking man with popping eyes fingered her between her ballooning cheeks. Once, and then again later, the kneeling woman jerked her head round and scolded the man: 'You're hurting, do be careful!' The man would wait a few seconds before moving his hand forward, squirming his finger into her again while she swayed and forced up her rump sensually. I was shocked. The seated couple kissed on inexhaustibly, and I saw a blob of spittle running down the woman's chin. Eyes closed, devoured by two mouths, she groaned something over and over again ecstatically. I could not catch what it was.

Osvaldo took my hand in a firm grip and I grew faint as he set me down on a couch heaving with cushions. I was trembling by now and quite incapable of speech.

Next to us, an athletic young man was making love to a woman, her face buried in his neck. With each potent thrust, she squealed 'Oh yes, more, oh yes, more' in a kind of litany.

The man's wet penis went back and forth in her splayed oval, which was starkly red like a wound. I could see absolutely everything!

Greedily I watched them nearing their climax. But I then forced my eyes away, to enjoy the breathtaking sight of the youth's bottom as it curved and relaxed, his crease spreading and clinching rhythmically. I had never seen this before. He was beautifully rounded and tight, and his thigh muscles pulsated as he gradually went faster.

I became aware of Osvaldo's fingers on my cheek. I shuddered at the touch.

'What about us, *tesoro*?' he whispered. There was something devilish about him.

I was so tense that I released an idiotic giggle, more of a bleat than a laugh. But already his hand had cupped my knees and was slipping under my dress. My own hands were none too steady.

Pushing him down, I blurted: 'Oh no, don't. Please, please!' I arranged my dress, it was awfully embarrassing.

'Come, my *tesoro,* you wouldn't play hard-to-get with your old friend Osvaldo?'

'No, I mean I can't do it now, not here.' But it was immediately clear that I would have to fight him off.

'Relax,' he persisted, 'it's so lovely with lots of people ...'

His hand was across my thighs, snaking up, and in no time at all he deftly slipped his fingers under my panty elastic.

31

'No, I don't like it, please Osvaldo, take me home. Please!'

I thought I could count on him, but I was wrong. In a swift movement he slipped my diminutive panties down to just above my knees, so that I was completely powerless to move. All men are the same.

Now another man was looming over me, more of a boy, taut and muscular like a Greek god. I simpered as his hands glided over my legs, warm and soft, his eyes deep and gleaming with desire. 'You are delicious, he murmured, 'so enticing.' I struggled to free myself from his tightening hold. I was so frightened.

Their four hands were caressing me. I was at their mercy, they removed my panties completely and my entire lower body instantly flamed. I tried to control my feelings but the youth's lips were upon my feet, my knees, nudging between my thighs. His ardent mouth drew closer and my pelvis leapt. With a supreme effort of will, I told myself it had to stop and I broke free, seized my panties and was on my feet, frantically rearranging my dress.

'I can't, Osvaldo,' I whimpered, my face scarlet. 'I have to leave.'

The two men stood back and I could see the youth's penis sticking out hard and thick, his face white with thwarted passion.

Glancing heavenward, Osvaldo turned to him and spread his arms like the Latin he was. 'Incredible,' he laughed with a jerk of the chin at me. The meaning was clear: 'Just like a woman!' The phallocrat!

It was well before dawn when I reached my studio-apartment, still fuming, and slammed the door. Damn the neighbours for once, they could go to hell. I flung myself onto the bed.

Hot tears welled up with the avalanche of recriminations that overcame me: 'Stupid bitch, silly little bourgeoise-schoolgirl-daughter-of-Mary. Afraid of sex, frightened at a prick, spoilsport, coward, scared to have an orgasm with a strange man.' I blubbed: 'And I wanted it so much.'

I was still living the youth's moist fleshy lips on my pubis, the entwined bodies of the couples as they wrestled, the exciting orange glow. I felt so humiliated, what a fool I had been.

He was on top of me, wanting me and I wanting him, I had only to yield. His hands were all over me, lusting for me. And his throbbing male-male-male penis that I was yearning for him to push in, even violently if he liked, vanquishing my resistance. Oh how I ached for it, was still aching for it!

But the poison of Sister Marie-Thérèse had done its work. 'Come along now,' she seemed to twitter, 'stop that now, it's wicked and sinful.' And like a naughty little girl I had blushed and run away, prisoner of purity and convent morality. Lord, what an idiot I'd been!

At length, still angered, I turned on my back. I found the hem of my dress and my fingers sought the moist relief I needed so urgently.

April 22

It was Angèle, our petite maid from Normandy, who really showed me how to obtain pleasure by myself.

She slept in a small room close to mine, and sometimes asked me to join her in her bed. She was afraid of the dark and we ought to sleep together. At least that is what Angèle said.

'Slip your nightie off,' she whispered one night. 'You'll be warm enough in my arms.'

She started fondling me after a while, just a little, and then showed me what she did to herself. I knew somehow it was naughty and I might get into trouble, but I looked at her for ages just the same. Later I began doing it to myself, and then often.

I did not mention it to Mummy until three or four years later, by which time Angèle had been gone for some time.

I was no different from most girls in our society, and even boys. My sexual awareness evolved in an abject way and I always had this dreadful feeling it was sinful.

I am still ashamed about the incident at *Le Bassano* and I suppose the fascination the youth held for me was similar to the curiosity I had towards Angèle. I am wondering if the pleasure you get isn't more intense if it is forbidden. The more 'wrong' it is the greater the excitement.

It seems to me that shutting your eyes to this so-called morality is a healthy reaction. It is the idea of wrongness, the ban on pleasure, that is so deeply morbid. At the same time it is thrilling.

But I am not sure what to think about that. I have not quite worked it out yet.

April 25

I chose Thursday evening for the most daring thing I had ever done. This is the evening when the upper classes tend to go out, rather than Friday or Saturday like the crowds. Thursday's people seem more positive.

The manager of *Le Bassano* peeked at me through the spyhole with a rather bloodshot eye, and I gave him my sweetest smile. The door opened at once, but the boss glanced out left and right to check on the passers-by. It was very secretive.

I hauled in Osvaldo and took him right past the bar without stopping. He was dragging his feet.

'*Tesoro*,' he exclaimed. 'Let's just have a little drink ...'

I tugged him into the orange room, and plonked him down on one of the couches. He seemed exhausted, and a little nervous.

'But my treasure ...'

Within seconds I slipped off my dress, kicked my shoes away, took down my panties and everything fell in a puddle under me. I went straight to the big bed in the middle and lay on my back. I opened my legs wide.

'Come on then,' I bubbled.

Osvaldo was stupefied, frozen into immobility. There was

a sudden hush in the room, the couples and groups of people stopped wriggling around and everyone looked at me in astonishment.

I suddenly felt scared. What did I imagine I was doing, for heaven's sake? I had got it all wrong and was being utterly ridiculous, and they all knew it. I wanted the earth to open up, wanted to die, it had gone wrong. The gesture was a complete farce!

I sought Osvaldo's eyes and saw he was grinning. It could still work, perhaps, in any case I had to go through with it now.

'What are you waiting for?' I threw out in a thick voice.

Not a soul moved, and I bit my lip. My heart was thumping, and I was in a state of panic.

I remembered a trick I used to use. It generally works and the horrors disappear and I regain control.

I pinched my right ear, deliberately relaxed, drummed my fingers. Then in this mute and half-clothed temple of Eros I quietly whistled 'The bridge over the River Kwai.' My legs are at 70 degrees, and I don't mean Centigrade!

To my infinite relief a man gets to his feet and begins walking around me. I bless him for it. I catch him by an arm unawares and pull him onto me, so that his whole weight is squashing me. I do not care that it is painful at first. Two more come up and I have all three, defiantly at first but with growing enjoyment. Then a woman's face is above mine, her hair falls over us and she strokes my neck and kisses me passionately. I lose count. They are handling my feet, stroking my hands, licking my ear, kneading my bottom. A large misshapen penis forces its way into my mouth and I feel the man's scrotum on my chin. A finger explores my anus, hurting me.

It is not funny any more and I am worried. I throw a desperate appeal at Osvaldo, but he just keeps watching, the swine! I am a squirming mass of flesh being pummelled, massaged, caressed, rubbed, scratched, pinched, bitten, penetrated again and again. I can feel urine trickling over my torso. I give myself up to this festival of erotica and I am lost in a whirl of bodies, rhythms, colours, acrid smells and semen.

How long I went on I have no idea. All sense of time forsook me. My body lost all feeling, I was drained of energy, flaccid from repeated orgasms. I felt like a sacrificed virgin.

At length I managed to stir and they were all standing around me, smiling down. They treated me royally, bending low to kiss my feet, gently cupping my hands. A man with greying hair, in his fifties and immensely handsome, signalled to me to sit up. I recognised him, he had penetrated me from the rear when I was face down in a particularly submissive posture. With incredible delicacy he took my hand and lightly applied his lips in princely fashion.

'*Mademoiselle*, you were magnificent.'

A woman clasped my face in her hands, and kissed my mouth lovingly through straying wisps of hair.

'You were beautiful, beautiful,' she told me.

The manager advanced, his pride taking years off him. 'Our little princess,' he whispered in my ear.

I was radiant, I had regained my self-respect, I was being worshipped. I was so happy!

'Come now, we're going home.' It was Osvaldo, his face as long as an old dishcloth.

Home in my studio-apartment, under a scorching hot shower, spraying my intimate parts in a cloud of perfumed steam, I yelled out an old French lovesong. The neighbours could go jump in the lake!

I felt like a million dollars. I was making up for lost time, having the kind of men I wanted, kicking over the traces, experiencing thrills and joys beyond my wildest dreams.

And this was only the beginning. The world was my oyster, nothing could hold me back now. I was heady with power over men!

April 27

The phone snatched me from the arms of Morpheus around 7 a.m. today. My face contorting in annoyance, I waded out of sleep and out of an exotic dream apparently in the West Indies. A black man glistening with sweat was kissing me on the beach, boats danced on the waves off-shore, and I was playing with his enormous shaft. It was a dream I was having repeatedly just before waking.

With a groan I reached for the receiver. A noise like the Valkyries in a drainpipe reached my tender ear. Osvaldo, I might have guessed.

'You've run out on me.'

'Huh?'

'You've simply let me drop.'

'Ah?'

'Why are you so stony-hearted with me?'

Bye bye black man, *au revoir* palm-trees, the soft white beach sinks into the ocean and I blink myself into reality.

Gentlemen should never ring ladies before 8 a.m., however worried they are about their rights over us. Osvaldo hasn't got over my little orgy of two nights ago. My lips form into a smirk, at least that's what it is intended to be.

When *he* took *me* to *Le Bassano* there was no difficulty. I was his property, his bird to be shown off, his plaything to be shared with his little friends before he collected me up and took me home from the party.

But on the second occasion, *I* was the one in charge, showing my independence, taking the initiative. His male pride was cut to the quick.

He now lectured me as if reciting from a document. Between the lines it went something like this: 'Sexual freedom is for men only, because we're men. It is not the same for women, it is not in their NATURE to be unfaithful. A woman's genitals are wrapped round her heart, but men are not made the same way. Men may copulate without love, whereas women may not.'

Not our nature, says the old pig! There is no such thing as

37

nature. There is the tragic history of women's slavery to men
century after century, bound hand and foot to the male. In
the opening years of the 17th century, an imbecile by the
name of Thomas Sanchez wrote: 'It is more in compliance
with the nature of things that men should act and woman
submit ... The natural copulatory position is for the woman
to lie on her back and the man to lie on her belly, ensuring
that he ejaculates into the receptacle intended for this use.'

How convenient for men that women's nature is thus.

Oh my sisters, poor weak women, wives, mistresses,
concubines! How much longer will your vaginas be the toys
of Man? Rise up and live your unbridled desires, do not fear
them, they can do you no harm!

Osvaldo, then, is perplexed at my little shindig at the club.
The poor wretch is now aware that he is NOT INDISPEN-
SABLE.

As the psychologists would say, I am wondering if his
phallus hasn't taken a knock or two.

He is crooning into the phone, pleading on his knees.

'*Tesooroo*,' he coos, 'try and understand ...'

I have had enough and I slam down the receiver. I get as
far as the bathroom, and he rings again.

This time he's the Flying Dutchman: '*TESORO*!'

'Mm?'

'Do you love me?'

'I'm not sure.'

'*Ma* what do you mean, you don't know?'

'Love, love, love, I don't know what it is. Maybe it's the
ultimate for poodles.' (I don't know what I mean either!)

'*Ma tesoro* ...'

'*Ma* what? What-what-what? Oh shit. *Basta cosi*!'

That's it. I switch the thing to the answering machine and
run myself a bath. As I flap my hand about making a big blue
foam, I can hear the machine clicking away, recording
message after message.

Smugly I realize that he cannot go on all day.

38

April 28

I cannot help wondering how I came to be emancipated so suddenly. How is it that I found the secret and could free myself of the constraints and seemly behaviour driven into me as a girl?

Few women have done as much. Their circumstances, their duties as married women, their life styles – everything divides us. They have remained 'respectable': I have become 'disrespectful' and I like it that way.

I certainly do not envy my two older sisters with their 'fine husbands', and now sliding steadily into a desperate conventionalism. How could I be jealous of the brilliant career opening up for Huberte after going through the E.N.A. Higher College of Administration? Administrators disgust me anyway. Cécile worries me too. Only two years older than I am, she is in her third year of Medicine, cramming night and day, learning by heart everything she will forget when the exam is over. There is little doubt that she is on the straight and narrow road to conformity, the trap all medical people fall into.

No indeed, I would not like to be in their shoes. There is less and less in common between us. I am creating my own revolution, or at least working out my evolution, while my sisters are battening down the hatches of conformist society.

My social status and mental balance are far harder to maintain than theirs. I am not travelling the smooth track of a career, and have no wish to. I refuse to go from A to B.

For me, at all events, if I am going to find my own way in life, I simply have to be sexually emancipated.

As to financial matters, these are secondary. I cannot throw money around, but I am not complaining. My monthly student's allowance is enough for me to get along with.

April 29

Madame Babarenskaya, my aged dancing teacher who

doesn't miss a thing, has noticed I have altered.

Today after a particularly gruelling session at the exercise bar, she took me aside.

'That was very good, Galia. You have perfect balance now, you possess more energy too. What is happening to you?'

'I can't imagine, Madame.'

'Come now, you are keeping little secrets. You can tell old Baba. You've fallen in love?'

'Oh no, on the contrary.'

'Whatever do you mean?'

'I am liberated.'

'Didn't it work out between you?'

'I am liberated less from a man than from the constraints and hang-ups of the past. I am discovering a new freedom.'

'Well, if it gives you wings, why not?' Very quietly she added: 'What hang-ups do you mean?'

'Moral hang-ups that had my body in thrall.'

April 30

Claude Terrois took me to dinner last night at *La Chaumière des Halles*. An excellent choice, a restaurant with a pleasant intimacy and impeccable service.

Claude's hand trembled when he took mine. I liked that. I do a quick mental recall on the Heymans and Wiersma type-classifications and wonder what Claude is: emotive-active-primary? While he is talking he keeps touching me, timidly with his fingertips, though rather mechanically. He is really rather sweet. His eyes are popping out of his head, he likes me, perhaps he is emotive-active-secondary. I am sure I ought not to keep on pigeon-holing people like this. After all, who cares whether they are primary or secondary? Claude is physically there across the table from me, he's nice, and that is all that counts.

Occasionally he stops chattering, gazes into my eyes, smiles and clenches my hand. I am famished, I feel great, and

I like males to want me, to spend money on me.

A bald penguin deposits a grilled turbot on our table and gives us a little bow. The turbot smells terrific. Another penguin uncorks a Pouilly Fumé with slick virtuosity, the cork making as much noise as a fly breaking wind. Penguin Number Two waves the cork under his nose and bats his eyes for a split second. Wordlessly, he pronounces it in good condition. As if we didn't know.

The dinner is perfect. Claude, whom I warm to increasingly as the minutes go by, has the good taste to discuss neither his work, nor money nor cars. This is rare in a man these days. He is an opera enthusiast. And yet he is not homosexual; my theory that all male opera lovers are homosexuals needs reappraising, I can see.

Turbot and Pouilly make a wonderful match. We are into our second bottle and the world looks more promising as the minutes go by. Strange how wine loosens me up.

It is rather quiet, the place is anything but crammed, and the lights are low. Claude is a good listener too, I notice. I'm the one who is running the conversation now, as the wine takes effect. Claude's cheeks seem to be giving off a mauve hue, and he suddenly declares: 'You know Galia, I find you intensely desirable.'

'Do you really,' say I, demurely.

Pushing off my right shoe with my left toe, I slowly extend my freed leg under the tablecloth, and it heads for the Terrois trouser zip. My brazen foot just reaches, if I slouch just a little in my chair.

The aforesaid Terrois turns a bright strawberry, and I breathe: 'But Claude, I thought men got big and hard. You are still soft, although I am touching you.'

'Oh but I desire you. Absolutely.'

'Show me how much, Claudie, show me you crave for me. I wish I had a thing like yours.' I am being so feminine. I pout and part my lips and signal my admiration for him as I apply the very slightest of pressure, then scoop him up slowly from below. He looks as if he might lift off at any moment.

What joy to feel his squashy genitals awakening, his organ swelling and then stiffening into a rod of iron! I feel a sense of power, and think it must be hurting him. If I had his thing I would be touching myself all the time to make sure it was still there; and then stroke it so that it stuck out proudly in front. It occurs to me that perhaps I ought to consult an analyst.

My own little volcano is starting to erupt, and I can feel that my gusset is wet. I hope it will not show through my skirt. Ah, the delectable instant of desire!

The thick white cotton tablecloth is aiding our thoughts, and we stay looking at it for a while. I am wearing cotton but Claude does not know. He would love to know what I am wearing.

Our penguin comes up with a list of desserts and an inscrutable look. 'Something to follow?'

'Oh yes,' I say, trying to frustrate Claude's rising lust. 'Something not too heavy, strawberries and cream perhaps? Lots of cream please, and lots of strawberries too. Do take your time, we are in no hurry.'

It's a lie, of course, we are both as hot as a couple of ants. Instead of waiting there, I take Claude's arm and lead him down to the toilet. He is ashamed of the hump in his trousers, hiding it with a napkin.

The walls are a lovely pink and so are the two washbasins. The mirrors have low lighting.

We can't wait an instant, we are holding each other tight now, our mouths wide open, our tongues fleshy and sloppy within. Our noses are bent, such is our haste. I feel so randy, but I prolong the pleasure! I simply nestle into his whole body for a moment, then I undo his zip and feverishly pull down his zip.

'Someone will see us,' he protests hoarsely. 'Anyone could come down.'

That is part of the thrill and I plunge my hand inside his underpants, and at last I am holding his big burning thing and feeling his testicles. I could pinch them and make him cry in pain. I squat down and take his penis hungrily into my mouth and he pushes it far into my throat. As I suck, Claude breathes faster and faster and I hope he won't come too soon. Another instant of penis-envy when I wish girls could have fellatio, then he seems to grow even bigger, and I lick his bulbous tip voluptuously. Claude is babbling incoherently.

Quickly, I pull him against me and step back against the wall. My cotton panties are down in a split-second and I glimpse the wet patch, but there is no time to lose. I lift my skirt up, with one arm I circle his waist, I spread my knees and with my other hand I guide him into my vaginal entrance. Almost at once we both explode in a frenzy and kiss to hide our cries.

Then we climb the stairs in a rose-tinted haze to eat our strawberries and cream.

May 2, 4 a.m.

The phone jerked me from sleep at two o'clock. It is Osvaldo.

'I am going to die.'

'Nonsense, you have years ahead ...'

'I tell you I am dying.'

His voice does sound weak, and I realize he is not bluffing. In an instant I am genuinely worried.

'Whatever have you done?'

No answer.

'Stay where you are, I'm coming over.'

Prostrate on the bed, Osvaldo is sighing half unconscious. I can hardly grasp what he is saying.

' ... rather die than live without you ...'

'What have you swallowed,' I demand. 'Quick, what was it?'

He cannot speak. Horrified, I see dozens of pill boxes in the bedclothes. My God, he must have taken them all!

I call an ambulance, and hold his hand until two white-coated men knock and hasten through the door which I left ajar.

'Is this the suicide?'

They took him away on a stretcher. His throat made a rattling noise going down the stairs. My eyes are smarting.

At the moment I can hardly control my hands, they are shaking so much, but I must get this down in writing. I haven't stopped trembling since the ambulance.

He is in the Hôtel-Dieu Hospital, but they would not allow me to stay. I can see him tomorrow.

May 2, 6 p.m.

They have put Osvaldo in a white room in a white bed with white bedclothes. He looks ghastly, but they cleaned out his stomach.

I start crying the moment I see him. I weep buckets, feel guilty, and he gazes up at me with infinitely desolate eyes.

'It's not the end of the world,' I whisper.

'Not the end, *tesoro*. Your hand.'

I place my hand in his and let him play with my fingers one by one.

'I cannot live without you, I can't.'

'And you can't think of a better way to tell me?'

'Perhaps it was the only way to show how much I love you.'

I stayed the rest of the morning. Around noon, I consented to a fortnight's 'trial marriage'.

May 3

Osvaldo is being sent home this afternoon.

Already I am concerned about giving in as I did, even though it is only a try.

I wonder if I am capable of having a fully-fledged relationship with a man, something that lasts and is on firm foundations. I tire of people so easily, my energies are too dispersed, I demand too much perhaps.

True, I like the idea of building a home, of two people as a permanent couple, but I cannot build brick by brick. I don't know how to plan things.

It is true as well that I feel the need for a shoulder to lean on, someone who has the answers to my many questions.

I need a lynchpin, a master. That is what I lack and I am beginning to realize it.

My affinity with Osvaldo has limits, is not well balanced. I am his mistress but he is no longer the master. The prospect of these two weeks fills me with misgiving.

It seems only yesterday that we first met. I was scarcely head over heels. But he was struck dumb when he saw me, or at least that's what he has claimed all this time.

It was at the George V Hotel, at a reception by a publishing house which was presenting some prize or other.

It was crowded, noisy, very Parisian, and people were practically fainting with the heat. Everybody kept moving around, forming small groups for a while, depending on the way the champagne and goodies came in and were placed on the buffet tables. They were writers, journalists, publishing people, radio, television and other personalities in the public eye. They were crying out things like: 'I'll give you a ring ... Let's have lunch next week ... No problem ... Have you read it, a superb book ... Chomsky with a touch of Rimbaud expressed in Alphonse Boudard's style ...'

All very stimulating, except for me.

'You seem abashed, my pretty maid,' a voice said.

He had approached unawares and now towered above me, slim and smiling. He looked old, 45 or even 50.

'On your own?' he went on.

'Ye-es.'

'In publishing?'

'No.'

'Journalism?'

'No.'

'Pirate radio perhaps?'

'No.'

'Legitimate radio, television?'

45

'No.'

'You don't give much away.'

'Sometimes.'

'Unlucky me. You know, you have the most striking eyes.'

'I know.'

'I-er-would you like some champagne?'

'Yes please. Could you also get me some of the sugary things? Especially the little green ones with chocolate on, and a few cream ice-cakes, and some pink thingamies with chocolate sprinkling, and the currants look good too. Oh, and don't forget some coffee eclairs and a dish of almonds.'

'Is that all?'

'Yes. No. I believe I saw some red ices, raspberry I think, but you'll have to ask, I only want raspberry. Those finger biscuits are nice too, and a few dates. Thank you, you're very thoughtful.'

He was gallant, eventually getting back to me loaded up and pushing through saying 'Sorry, sorry.' We sat down under a sunshade on the *terrasse* outside where it was quiet.

'Allow me to introduce myself. Osvaldo Salvatori.'

'Galia S ...'

'An unusual first name. You yourself are mysterious. You are ravishing, in fact. Tell me how you got into this Noah's Ark.'

'I have a girl friend in publishing, and she got me an invitation because I wanted to meet René Giard.'

'The philosopher?'

'Yes, but he hasn't turned up.'

'Why him?'

'He has brains.'

'He has indeed. But what do you like in him?'

'Those green things please. Thanks. A complete in-depth scrutiny of the entire spectrum of Western mythical theologies ...'

'You are at the faculty?'

'I'm reading Thai for languages. I have dancing lessons too.'

He let me go on, talking about my childhood in Tours, the family, my sisters. He certainly knew how to listen. Most people cannot, they just wait until they can get their sentence in. Osvaldo struck me as charming, warm of character, interested in others. Afterwards he told me his life story, about his children including one older than I was, his divorce, his job as a producer in T.V.

Then out of the blue he took my hand and raised it to his lips, elegantly.

'Are you already in love?' I mocked.

'Yes.' He looked at me openly, eagerly. 'And aren't you in love, just a teeny bit?'

'No.'

'Well, that's clear enough ... Might we meet again, d'you think?'

'Yes.' He had said it with such refinement.

'When?'

'Would you like to take me to dinner?'

'I would enjoy it immensely, Galia.'

'Tomorrow then?'

'So be it.'

'I won't sleep with you, Osvaldo.'

'Oh come, please, I had absolutely no intention ...'

'Yes you had.'

'Galia, you are diabolical. Of course, I want you. You are so very beautiful.'

And he made me believe it, taking me out to plays, to the cinema, playing tennis. But not to *Le Bassano* yet. I was still rather gauche. Soon he was phoning me every day, then several times a day. He would meet me at the faculty.

One evening after a kiss that went on and on, I almost let him take advantage of me, I felt something hard between our bodies, but I was still a virgin and scared so told him it was time he left. I was sorry at once and phoned to apologize. Within minutes he was back! We lay down together on my bed, I let him pet me and I responded timorously. But my

47

defences were strong and I resisted the temptations closing in on me.

Until the great day at the tennis courts, when I became his 'mistress', as they say. He became my teacher, showing me everything about my body, everything I was missing.

Osvaldo had experience, he was a woman's man, and it was natural that he should initiate me. I was fortunate, I have to admit.

He was so patient, helping me overcome my inhibitions, he was kind and skilled, he respected me. He knew the virtuosity of a woman's body, the feminine psychology, how women reacted and what they wanted. He obtained immense pleasure from teaching me.

Other men I encountered seemed so awkward and unsure of themselves and selfish and crude. From the outset Osvaldo showed concern over my enjoyment. It was another victory for him every time he brought on an orgasm. At first when we made love I was slow to rouse, my libido seemed to hesitate. Those awful Ursuline nuns had really got me uptight.

I shall always be grateful to Osvaldo for giving me a comprehensive course in pleasure!

May 4

Osvaldo is his old cheerful self again, and as a surprise he is flying me to Haiti.

To tell the truth, this trip is too much of a honeymoon for my liking. He has obviously forgotten his suicide. I haven't.

'What's done is done,' he says rather too often to be comfortable. He is grinning like a sandboy about the future, but in my case it transpires that things are not so happy ever after.

He means well and Haiti could be quite an experience.

May 5

I am writing this on a plastic tray affixed to the plane seat in front of me, where a fellow passenger is snoring like a warthog. It is 11 p.m. Paris time, 6 p.m. New York time. We are in the Paris-Miami Boeing 747, all of us holidaymakers.

We have been chasing the sun for hours now. It is sinking endlessly in reddish blue space as we advance on it. It's strange, a sunset that lasts for ever.

Osvaldo is sleeping like a child beside me. Everyone has settled into the routine, dozing and dreaming with their eyes open, music plugged into their ears (choice of 8 soundtracks).

I pity the fatties, there isn't much room in these seats. In fact, it is my opinion that the aeroplane is the most uncomfortable as well as the most convenient means of transport in this day and age. The Air France boffins have counted every cubic centimetre, and try to apologize for it with slick stewards and friendly hostesses. I have a feeling it doesn't actually catch on.

The horizon is now blood red and the setting sun is getting on my nerves. The plane is trying to catch up time, and I am going to catch up on some sleep, hand in hand with my beloved. We are in mid-Atlantic and I am a weeny bit afraid.

May 6

The Olofson Hotel at Port-au-Prince is a splendid plantation-style timber residence surrounded by a botanical garden. Only it's for real.

It certainly gives you the creeps, it's romantic and magical at the same time. It could be the relative humidity or the voodoo or the screaming horrors. When I first set foot on Haiti I knew we were in a spooky triangle.

Christopher Columbus sailed into Ayti (in Arawak language it means 'high wild land') and cried out: *'Es una maravilla!'*

Well alright, it was marvellous. But the Spaniards still conquered and looted it. The peaceloving Arawak Indians, who worshipped the moon, the sun, the stars and the springs

49

of water, welcomed the navigators with armfuls of gifts. They were promptly decimated, and new manpower had to be brought in from Africa. Haiti got blacker and blacker, and erstwhile Hispaniola is now more like Africa than the West Indies.

The official language here is French, but the natives speak Creole.

A kid at the airport asked me: 'You American madam?'

'No, me French,' I replied huffily.

'You madam France. Is good.'

The low-lying land that used to be marshy is still called Limonade and Marmelade. The villages have names like Belle Dondon, Marie-Galante and Saltrou (dirty hole!).

The buses in Port-au-Prince are rainbow-coloured and they carry nick-names like 'Mary's Son', 'Thy Will Be Done' and 'Little Jesus of Paris'.

May 7

I am sipping a Planter's Punch on the edge of the pool at the Olofson, and the aroma is going to my head. Osvaldo has gone to see an exhibition of primitive Haiti paintings. I go more for peace and quiet, for lazing around and voluptuous daydreams.

Occasionally there is a splosh noise when someone dives in, a guest titters politely. The people here seem amazingly respectable, mostly Americans from the world of art. A few homosexuals, I notice. Ten yards from me one of them aged about 25 is working hard at his tan, with a kind of silver drip-plate round his neck to reflect the sun. How he can stand it in this heat is a mystery.

My Planter's Punch is pretty hot and, unless it's the Haiti spirits, it gives me an overpowering urge to make love, to copulate like some wild beast, to go crazy, to (this is my private diary after all) have a damn good fuck. I want a big prick fucking me hard right inside. I'm being vulgar but perhaps just writing it down in this impulsive way will reduce

50

the ache, sublimate the desire. Not a hope, there is nothing I can do about it. The sun is wickedly hot and so am I!

May 7, 6 p.m. with T'i Punch

I am progressing, becoming bolder, the taboos are falling away.

This morning I had to have a man, any man, even a fool, provided he could get a whacking great hard on. I looked around, searching for one. Alongside the pool there were some quite eligible males, at first sight that is. But it's hardly the thing to go up to a deck chair and say: 'Excuse me, please. I simply can't wait to get it off, how about a quickie?'

And what if the deck chair doesn't like girls? What if he doesn't want it? Or I'm not his type? How humiliating! I might even pick a homo without realizing it and he might screech out in his fruity voice: 'Oh how awful, d'you know what she just said to me?'

So I play it clever, I want a fuck, but I have my self-respect too. My eyes stray around the pool, watching for a prick at the ready.

I've got one at last! Just what I need. I rivet my eyes on the bulge in his bathing trunks, and I think he hardens up just a little, enough to show he could be thinking on similar lines. Tough luck on us girls, we can't signal it physically, only with our attitude. Our panties grow moist but it doesn't show. How I would love to stroll round the pool, proud and upstanding, my little slip straining in front, scarce concealing my blood-filled chopper! I might stiffen so much, the purple tip would burst out over the top.

He is a tall blond lad, fairly stocky with a gorgeous tan. But my whole attention is concentrated on his 'cobra'.

Oh Galia, how lubricious you are becoming, how lewd! Not entirely, I tell myself, but I am working on it. These days I am more interested in the phallus than the man behind it, than his soul. But maybe pricks have souls too.

The beautiful cobra is lying in his nest waiting to spring,

51

only the nest is a tight 75% cotton 25% polystyrene, iron at 80°C max.

I slink over without overdoing it, and see he is reading *Newsweek*. It looks like a dull week by his expression, and I stare at his shiny trunks, telling him as loud as I can: 'You have a superb cobra, you know.'

What he actually hears is: 'Have you been here a long time?' In English.

'Only a week. Are you French?'

'Yes I am.' I am pretty vexed at this, I thought I had a perfect accent.

'Fine, well have a drink.'

We're off on the first straight. But how many minutes will we have to sniff around? I can't wait, but we keep on at it. Yes Haiti is a fascinating island, no it's my first visit, yes I flew via Miami, no I haven't been to Jacmel yet, yes I'd love to see La Citadelle. For pity's sake, it's your cobra I want to see! How long is it, how thick, how often does it strike?

They need a while to turn on, these Americans. Take it easy, take it easy, buddy, OK. But I'm in a hurry, I can feel my vulva gaping. I step on the gas and tell my cowboy: 'I'd like to show you something.'

'Ok,' he says. 'I'll be right back, just gonna put something on.'

How dumb can you get? Do I have to spell it out? Have I roped a bum steer?

He gives me a smile as clean as a church pew and goes into a changing hut at the end of the garden in the shade. I wait a whole 30 seconds and then give a light tap on the door.

'Who is it?'

'It's me, open up.'

'I can't, just a minute.'

'Open the door NOW!'

He eases back the door and I give it a hefty shove. I shut it behind me. I am reaching boiling point, we are alone just the two of us in the blessed cool of the changing hut, and he still doesn't catch on. He looks at me with his doleful eyes, and I see that 30 seconds was just right. All he has on is one sock, but he hides himself like a clown behind his towel.

I snatch off my two-piece, remove his towel and press the whole length of my body against his. It's heavenly, so warm and sweaty, so thrilling that I get it off instantly just leaning against him.

I close my eyes and feel the second one coming. This one I have to have! It's lifting me up like a wave and my vagina is pulsing.

I am wrestling with a bull, I massage his biceps and chest; Osvaldo would weep with jealousy to see his mounds of muscle. I am bringing him on, I grope him and clench him and kneel and lick the longest and thickest and hardest organ I have ever seen. It is purple, jerking frantically. Then it pumps and pumps, the hot semen spurting warm on my face. He is moaning and gasping deliriously. 'Oh you bastard,' he croaks, and I don't know whether he means me or him. I don't care, he loves it!

Words of love, words of hate, poor words meaning nothing as we rush together into the Palace of Pleasure.

'Aw you dirty bitch, I love you, you bastard,' he mouths. Oh the divine language of pleasure!

He has not actually penetrated me yet, and I want that to be my third orgasm. His whopper is floppy now, and I wonder if I can get him up again; there are different opinions about that, but I set to work again. In a couple of minutes I have him ready, I am delighted with myself. It must be instinct, or the call of my own drenched sex.

Incredibly his dark red organ seems even bigger, and I can see only one way we can do it. I turn round, splay my hands against the opposite wall of the hut, and present my rump to him, legs apart. He enters me roughly, and I can feel him coming further and further, I wonder if it will ever stop penetrating, and then he withdraws, then thrusts again and again. In and out, in and out, like a piston, bumping me up and down. My orgasm bursts, filling my whole lower torso, and I sink to my knees heaving and gasping uncontrollably. I can hear the bull snorting wordlessly, and we stay like that in a state of exhaustion.

'What's your name,' I rasp.

'Steve.'

'Mine's Galia. See you later Steve.'

'Be seeing you, kid.'

May 8, 6 p.m. T'i Punch

As a matter of principle I hate telling lies. Lies are for people who will not say: 'It's like that, do what you like about it.' I am against evasiveness and concealment.

I tried to tell Osvaldo about it, but every time I was about to say 'You know this afternoon I made love with an American' he said something else. It could be he suspected something, but was unwilling to face the truth. I gave up. We have no right to inflict truths on those who do not want to know.

We strolled round the extraordinary Marché aux Fers at Port-au-Prince.

The Haitians are inventive because they are poor, cutting out shapes of men, women and animals from old jerrycans. The results can be strikingly artistic.

But the waves of tourists have spoiled this creative process, and what you get can be very cheap. It is still possible to pick up good work, but you need tenacity.

Osvaldo buys me an erotic allegory, highly 'macho'. The Women's Lib people would gnash their teeth in rage; in the foreground is a smiling man with an erection, in the background a woman in the jungle amid snakes and birds.

Painting is fairly new to Haiti, dating basically from 1944 when the official Art Centre was set up. Some 30 painters decided to 'create' a Haiti style deriving from African sculpture and Egyptian art. André Breton, they say, was immensely keen on the work of the best-known primitive painter here, Hector Hyppolite, who headed the so-called Marvellous Realism School.

These primitives are rather moving: very simple, full of light, flat and with no perspective.

May 9, 6 p.m. T'i Punch and bird calls

Petit Pierre has the best set of primitives on the island, at his villa-cum-gallery overlooking Port-au-Prince. People come from all over the world to see this legendary character.

He is a fine figure of a man, as my mother would say, in spite of his small stature. His skin is a lovely West Indian brown and he is elegant in dress, speech and movement. His eyes sparkle at the sight of a good painting or an attractive woman.

Petit Pierre showed us some of his best paintings, and a collection of tin work to take your breath away.

We had dinner outdoors in the warm air with exotic plants all around us.

Petit Pierre and Osvaldo found they had common friends in New York as well as Paris. It's a small world, they rightly decided. They meant the world of art; I cannot imagine a tourist from Citroen meeting an Italian and crying out: 'Good grief, you know Arturo from Fiat too!' There is a world of cultural freemasonry.

Of course, Petit Pierre proved vastly informed on the paintings of Haiti. He once lectured the French cultural godfather André Malraux when he visited the island. But I don't think he played footsie under the table with Malraux like he was doing with me.

The three of us went dancing at a place with a round floor, a circle of coloured lights and palm-trees waving against the night sky. We swung our hips to the magical West Indian band. Petit Pierre is an expert dancer, and has a romantic way of holding his partner: viz, his right leg welded to her crotch! He smiles artfully and so do I, his not-so-petit prick rolling back and forth across my navel or thereabouts. He knows I am getting clammy where his leg is, and increases the pressure.

55

Yes, Petit Pierre is horny enough to sweep any young girl off her feet. I have never slept with a black man.

May 10

La Citadelle Laferrière, built in the early nineteenth century by the 'Mad Emperor' Christopher, is a gaunt fortress perched 2,500 feet above the sea. Lindberg said it was the eighth wonder of the world. Whatever he thought about it, I was impressed.

Christopher, known as the black pharaoh of Cape Haiti, wanted to imitate the court of France's Louis XIV with everyone in fancy dress, sumptuous buildings including the Palais de Sans-Souci (Carefree Palace), bewigged officials, chamberlains, masters of ceremony, even 'Ducs de Limonade'. A former slave, he really weighed into his subjects, working them literally to death. He had the Citadelle built high up on its rock by teams of 100 men each. Once, on his orders, a bronze cannon weighing several dozen tons was hauled to the summit. A hundred slaves sweated blood as they struggled to get this goddam lump of bronze to the top. They collapsed halfway up, and he sent in a squadron of troops to shoot them. Another work-team stood by and was told: 'Now it's your turn.' In all, thousands of men perished in the construction of this stark cloud-ringed fort.

We went up on emaciated mules, by a narrow path. At every turn there were kids trying to sell us flutes, necklaces, bracelets and other things they made. I liked their smiles.

We got there at last and surveyed the grandiose sight. The fort is a stone palace hanging silent and deserted between the sky and sea. Mist wrapped itself round us and we shivered a little. I drew closer to my man, glaring at dozens of guns pointing out to sea. My mind flashes back to a book I read as a little girl. But in the case of the Citadelle, the invader never arrived and the blood and sweat was for nothing.

May 11. *Terrasse of the Olofson, Planter's Punch, bird calls, 7 p.m.*

For the first time in my life a man made me cry out with pleasure today.

Petit Pierre, clever guy, sent Osvaldo to see one of his fellow collectors at Jacmel this afternoon. In other words he had me all to himself for hours on end, and I speculated on how he would go about seducing me. Jubilantly he unrolled his favourite canvases one after the other, and I tried to concentrate on them.

At length he said: 'That's Marat at his best. What he did afterwards, the stuff at the New York galleries, was nothing compared to this!'

I found he was coming round to the point rather too slowly, and to help him I declared: 'Petit Pierre, I want you too. Let's do it now.'

His bedroom turned out to be cheerfully chaotic: paintings of course and articles of clothing, tinwork, books, newspapers, a typewriter with piles of finished sheets of paper. A mosquito net was draped round the bed, turning it into an old-fashioned cradle. He lowered me into the cradle, and I regarded him meekly.

What followed was a new kind of pleasure. He was electrifying, each of his kisses wherever he embraced me enhanced the intensity of my joy. I mean it. His lips, fingers and tongue explored me between my toes, under my feet, behind my ears, the backs of my knees, inside my elbows, the nape of my neck, round my waist, inside my thighs. He was adoring me, and the sensation it gave me revealed a new dimension in fervour. My sex gradually lost its tightness, and I knew he could do anything he liked with me and I would proffer no resistance. I really cannot put it into words. I remember only that I imagined myself to be a lovely pomegranate, erotic and feminine, opening out as the sun shone upon me. He made me feel so beautiful, and I worshipped him for that.

I spread my legs offering my most intimate self, my soul.

With infinite delicacy he gave tribute to my loins and my bottom. He licked me and gave me little bites, caressed me and drank my juice.

I exclaimed my ecstasy, although I tried to be quiet and was biting my upper lip. I can hear myself crying out but can do nothing about it.

I am completely out of control, lifted up in confusion, folly, triumph. I am eternal. I do not even think whether or not I am having an orgasm. It was all one.

We made love a second time, and it was another journey among the stars. Oh, the sheer delight of soaring into the firmament!

I learned now that in my own country across the Atlantic, Valéry Giscard D'Estaing has been beaten in the fight for the Presidency by the socialist François Mitterrand.

Politics have always seemed a silly show to me, but I admit to a certain satisfaction at seeing Giscard's arrogance at an end. At least we shall see some new people, hear some new voices. Everything is going to change, they tell us.

May 12, diary time and T'i Punch time (stronger than Planter's)

I had forgotten about the cowboy. He found me this morning as I lay on my cushions at the edge of the pool. I was reading a book about a hundred years of solitude. He picked the wrong moment, that's for sure.

'Hullo baby!'

'Oh, hullo Steve.' (Where did you spring from? And you're chewing gum too, for God's sake. And you look like a mental defective.) 'How are things?'

'I'd like to show you something, Galia,' he says with a wink straight out of MGM's studios.

He shifts his foot and then the other, and moves his hand past his great American cobra. A little hint that he wants some shooting practice.

58

'I'm so sorry, Steve. I don't want to – er – move for the moment.'

Good Lord, he thinks I haven't caught on, and repeats it: 'I'd like to show you something, something pretty.' He gives me an Uncle Tom smile.

Look here, buster, I want to say, I've had my dose for a while. Now take your big gun someplace else. Instead I moan: 'I want to be alone.'

Miraculously he starts to get the message. He makes a face: 'No jig-jig today?'

'No jig-jig today.'

'Tomorrow maybe?'

'Tomorrow maybe. So long Steve.'

Like kids they are. He'll just have to find another playmate, or do his own thing. Bye-bye Steve, you have a super cobra, but you are too dumb for words.

I am writing this on the marvellous Olofson *terrasse*. It is like being in a novel. The decor, the atmosphere, the characters, the noises and aromas are all so romantic. This old hotel is magic too.

Osvaldo has come and gone, giving me a touch on the cheek and telling me we are dining with R.A. and the French Ambassador, who by the way is said to be a total cretin. Osvaldo has taste, the tact to leave me alone when I am writing my diary.

Our relationship is calm and without incident. He knows this little birdie is touchy and may fly off if there is too much disturbance. It's one of Galia's bitchy days today.

May 13

The dinner was mortifying, in other words deadly dull. The French Ambassador bears one of our country's most illustrious names, and makes sure everyone knows it.

Poor France, for the man is a pretentious ass, the perfect example of the peevish old reactionary clutching onto his privileges for dear life.

59

Babies are dying by the hundred in the streets of Port-au-Prince, amid general indifference, and he observes: 'Death is something these people are used to ...' How does he know, the silly old fool? Life is crystal clear for our Ambassador. On the one side there are the decent people, the aristocrats, the elect (God's, not the voters') the nobility. On the other side is the rest of the human race, also known as horse-shit.

This particular member of the nobility has a face like a pig, a degenerate body, the brains of a sheep and horrible breath. But he also has this name, and that's why other top people treat him like God Almighty.

The meal goes on and on. Like a well brought up young lady I keep still and do not fidget, smiling politely as I imagine myself pouring the sauceboat over his head.

Politeness, decency, cowardice, what's the difference? Osvaldo and I leave the dinner feeling we want to scratch ourselves and take a shower.

It is around midnight and in the centre of Port-au-Prince 12-year-old children are making signs to the car drivers, under the soulless gaze of the bodyguards outside the palace of President-for-Life Claude Duvalier. For a handful of small change, a grown-up can buy a child's body for an hour.

Much of the city's population spends the night in the streets, not for the fresh air, but because they have no home. Haiti is the poorest country in the world. The per capita income is lower than in the least developed country of Africa.

May 14

Petit Pierre shows us some of the best-guarded treasures he has at his house.

While Osvaldo is turning over the visitors book on the *terrasse,* P.P. beckons me down to the cellar where he has stored a mass of paintings and valuables. Naturally, he jumps me while we are there. It is a high-speed knee-trembler surrounded by colourful bric-à-brac. He takes me standing up, which cuts the effort to a minimum for both of us as he is just about my height. We are like a pair of vertical rabbits, it is short but sweet – or rather bitter-sweet as the climax for me comes with a rush and seems to sting me. As always after intercourse, I feel refreshed. The fellow who wrote *post coitum omne animal triste est* was talking through his backside. Another negative moralist.

A few years ago at the age of 16 I would have fallen madly in love with Petit Pierre. Today I am less inclined to equate love and sex. This man has given me more pleasure than any other, he drives me crazy, but I am not in love with him. Just terribly fond of him.

I have never said 'I love you' to a man, even in the whirlwind of close embrace, even when I am out of my mind with excitement. I have never actually said 'my darling' either.

Something is missing, perhaps I am inhuman, but that is the way it is and I cannot help it. One day I may fall completely in love with a man, but this is still only a dream.

One of Petit Pierre's friends took us to a voodoo ceremony.

To the thrum of three drums, a splendid woman shimmies in a white garment. Bells are tinkling. She turns round and round, squats, leaps and sways. Suddenly she halts in front of me and signs to me. I turn to our friend, who signals me to stay where I am. The priestess persists. Distinctly embarrassed, I shake my head. Then she looks around and rushes at a tall heavy man, hits him and he goes down rolling in the dust.

The 'Loa' spirit has taken possession of the woman, or more accurately she has become the spirit. The spirit is riding her body and the 'Loa' laughs, insults, threatens, encourages, reveals the past and the future, feels no pain when walking on coals of fire.

Voodoo is indeed a dancing religion that is practised among friends and often in public. The possessed woman thrashes about in a frenzy, staggers, sweats, gasps for breath, starts it all over again. Then she stops brusquely, gazes around her in amazement, apparently emerging from a dream.

Our friend told us she would remember nothing of it all.

May 16

We left Haiti today and I feel disconsolate. We are turning our backs on the world of magic and returning to technology and all the other 'ologies' of civilized Man.

A short stay on Martinique. Fort-de-France makes me think of a Paris suburb in the tropics. A grim stopover, showing us a clear example of a country being wrecked by so-called civilization.

May 19, Paris

We have been back about two days and I feel awful. Uneasy, without bearings, incapable of thinking, losing control.

The Parisians are strange beings, frowning and scurrying about. Is it me or them on the wrong planet?

I wander from room to room in Osvaldo's apartment, opening the fridge, nibbling odds and ends without appetite, watching T.V. but registering nothing.

I feel depressed, alone.

May 20

I was looking through the magazine *Le Nouvel Observateur* and came across the personal ads. Click! I feel better already.

What a great idea! Meeting new people, making dates with strangers, launching out into the Unknown!

I do three or four drafts, and at last the ad is how I want it:

> **Girl, 20, attractive, liberated, seeks partners for love, fantasies, affection. No jokers, fogeys or flops. Tel ... photo preferred. Write box no . . .**

May 23

Already a dozen replies. The first letter I open is in jumpy handwriting and is from a psychiatrist. It is tumultuous, breathless.

Paris, May 22, 1981
Dear liberated friend,
I am 33, good-looking, physically in excellent shape,
passionate and enthralling, cultivated, tuned-in when
necessary and tender at times, and I am looking for an
attractive girl like you!
I am a practising psychiatrist, likable and easy to
get on with, without false modesty, carrying out
fascinating and absorbing work with adolescents, major
research and other responsibilities, and am therefore
personally concerned with everything to do with
adolescence.
I would like to meet you and suggest you phone
491.32.52 lunchtime and ask for Dr Yves Noroit.
Until soon, I hope. Best wishes.
(Signature like a pile of worms).

The second envelope contains a two-page magazine called *La Gazette Coquine* (The Saucy Gazette), with the sub-title 'The magazine of scandalous ads: hundreds of ads to take your breath away'. The contents include some photos the size of postage stamps.

A 042 – Age 50, virile, seeks women of any age if noisy spicey sluts.

The photo shows him standing nude with a towel over one shoulder. I can't see his face properly, but his appliance is impressive and was probably titivated before the picture to enhance its image.

A 043 – Perverted vicious couple seek sub-

missive male to bow to their demands. (No photo)

A 044 – (photo of stunning appetizing girl standing up). Lovely 35-year-old, refined, curvaceous, hyper-sensitive, managerial position with little time to spare, rich in money but poor in sperm, seeks discreet Paris meetings with men 25–49 strong and healthy, able to make love several times with ejaculations. No mouth caresses. Telephone an advantage.

A 045 – (No photo). Gentleman transvestite with liking for women's sexy underwear seeks men or women so that he can live out his fantasies. Lingerie worn during lovemaking.

A 029 – (Head and shoulders of fine bronzed man, athletic and smiling). Tall, slim and highly authoritarian, I seek willing slave accepting all humiliations and obeying all my commands. He will wash me daily with his tongue. Gentlemen interested write me now for detailed programme of what awaits you.

A 030 – (No photo, no indication of sex). I am 23, have a capricious mouth and lovely posterior. Seek young man my age liking love and laughter. No married men. (It must be a woman!)

A 003 – Is there a man who can make my brunette wife with a fine arched back happy? Priority accorded to imaginative people.

A 050 – Youth, virgin back and front, seeks girl or boy to deflower him.

A 028 – Young woman, plain but expert, likes perverted touching with strangers, accepts all rendezvous in porn cinemas.

A 017 – (Woman standing nude, over 40, heavy with big breasts). Young woman (sic) 46 inch bosom seeks man who appreciates large breasts. I like my nipples sucked for long periods and lovemaking between breasts. I come when you knead my breasts. (Oh, the cow!)

The publishers tell me on the bottom of the page that if I subscribe today for only 60 francs to *La Gazette Coquine* (supplied in plain, highly discreet wrapper), I shall receive a SURPRISE with the hundreds of small ads.

On page 2 I can request for 50 francs a secret map of the BOIS DE BOULOGNE indicating its extraordinary NOCTURNAL ORGIES. The Bois is enormous, I learn, and it is very difficult at night to know WHERE TO GO in order to SEE or PARTICIPATE in PARTIES and EXPOSURES of the most AUDACIOUS kind. The 50 francs buys me a DETAILED PLAN giving the precise location of each SPECIALITY or PERVERSION:

1. RENDEZVOUS and departure point for SEX PARTIES: this is where 90 per cent of the GROUP SEX in Paris begins each night. Stop by, just in case, newcomers always needed and taken care of.
2. LONE EXHIBITIONIST WOMEN: usually young bourgeoise ladies ON HEAT, trying to bring their FUTURE PARTNERS to a paroxysm of excitement.
3. NYMPHOMANIACS SUPPLIED NAKED by their husbands: many gentlemen in a state of fatigue wish to hand over their young

wives to groups of vigorous men; note a pronounced taste for MASOCHISM in these women.

4. PEEPERS: certain men and women exhibitionists generously reveal their MOST SECRET DEPTHS, enabling all peepers standing around to GET WORKED UP and GET IT OFF without FEELING ASHAMED.

5. NUDE TRANSVESTITES: you will see superb breasts, making the most beautiful women green with envy. FELLATIO GUARANTEED.

6. HOMOS: One of the major meeting points and HOMO SWAP CENTERS of Paris.

7. WHORES: almost always NUDE under a COAT, EXCEPT IN SUMMER; they will meet your every DESIRE for a few francs.

8. MALE PROSTITUTES: love-sick women give small PRESENTS to enjoy the virile attributes of horny young men. Try your luck.

9. DOMINATING WOMEN: if you are a masochist, here are STRONG-ARM women who are VERY CRUEL and will submit you to the worst outrages.

Immediately under this line is depicted a huge pair of scissors, but I am relieved to see they are for cutting out the coupon! For 50 francs the Bois de Boulogne belongs to you.

Here follows a SPECIAL OFFER FROM AUNTIE PORN: the 200-page SEX POCKET BOOK, a collection of ultra-perverse and scandalous photos selected by Auntie Porn.

Having perused this attractive journal in depth, I open some more letters. Fortunately they are not junk mail and they are hand-written.

Lovely boy, 30, likes liberated girls and unusual ads,
would love to meet you.
Jean-Paul Dessirer, *early morning or late evening.*

Gérard, 38, brown hair and slim, 5 foot 9 inches,
bachelor, attentive and sensitive, hungry and passionate,
adores Mozart and trees, youth, love, beauty, is unable

*to resist the temptation to reply to you. He is Parisian
like you, between journeys and weekends, and will do his
best to make our meeting richly promising in mutual
wonders.
Hoping to hear the music of your voice at an early date,
he submits his destiny to your pretty hands.
G. Fontenay, 742.21.71.
(Pleasant writing, large and leaning right. Impression of
balance. Very readable signature, vertical not
underlined.)*

The next letter, fast writing, small controlled lettering,
readable signature is very small.

*Dear Unknown,
You seek the ideal man, I am one of them. If we are
speaking of this same Adonis, you are the siren with
green eyes, auburn-haired, slender, tall. (Alas this is not
me at all, but let him draw the portrait.) You know how
to appreciate fine things, your judgement goes beyond
culture, travel has made you an artist, reading makes you
a poet (he has too much gab), you are not content just to
live your life, instead you create it. (what does he mean?)
I am a crazy lover of life, I have no taste for solitude. I
invite you to share the day-to-day, laborious early
mornings and tender evenings (hold on! This
programming worries me). We shall have our own lives
together, calm without excess, sometimes mad, always
tender. Marriage not obligatory (thank goodness for
that!), children are wanted, etc. etc.*

The home I have is closer to the pelvis. This noble lad is
afraid of overdoing it, so he can find a herb lady. Into the
trash-can with *La Gazette Coquine*.

The next missive looks rather promising, it's nicely
penned.

Hullo,
In the garden of my heart there is lots of room to play
and roll over in the wool of my veins (oh boy!) There is
a place for you too, little kitten, I think. A place for
imagination, all improvisations. And a little room for
entrechats and tender frolics. To gambol, laugh and have
fun in life it needs two, and the kitten has to be tender,
the tomcat attentive, and each heart must open with
discretion for the enjoyment of the other.
A meeting, a look, smile, adventure, life – all is possible.
Youth is the most precious of treasures, and alone it
allows everything to be created, everything to be
understood and achieved.
I am passionately interested in Chinese medicine and, if
you are not an adept, you are warned that you may be
converted. The other side of my life . . . from my whole
body, my aspirations and what makes me happy and
gives me pleasure.
Dear friend, I yearn to meet you if your heart responds
to mine, to exchange or taste each of the sources that
give us life.
I should be delighted to meet you one evening, how you
wish since it is you who are extending the invitation.
Loic Renaud, *aged 30*

In contrast with this polite and lyrical letter, the next
missive comes as a shock.

Dear little liberated cat,
I sniff you through your advertisement, my nose goes
right to its target and my tongue is licking you already
and you are wriggling a bit and you like it and you are
getting moist.
I caress you for a long time and you can stand it no
longer and you tell me 'come'.
I am well-equipped (10 inches deployed) and I know how
to use it. See you soon.
Hubert, *548.30.17*

In the Far West pictures, the boys spin their colts before they put them smoking into their holsters (i.e. vaginas). This expansive cowboy intrigues me. I grab the phone and ring 548.30.17. This I have to see!

'Hullo, my name's Galia.'

'Excuse me, who?' A strong deep no-nonsense voice. The fellow has no time to lose.

'I put the ad in.'

'Ah, little liberated cat! When can we get together? How about six o'clock?'

'Six tonight?'

'Yes, six to eight.'

'Well, I . . .'

'Right, that's settled. You come to my place. Know Rue Christine, 5th *arrondissement*?'

'I think . . .'

'I'm at No. 8, there's an intercom, ask for Hubert. Until then, 6 o'clock.'

Pretty off-hand, that runt, with his 10-inch pistol. It can't be true, 10 inches is a lot of Mars bar, worth going just to see that.

I have a yen to contact the psycho, Yves Noroit, the one who examines adolescents.

'Dr Noroit, yes,' he snaps.

'How do you do, my name is Galia, I'm the girl who put a small ad in *Le Nouvel Observateur* . . .' Complete silence, and I add: 'Can you hear me?'

'Yes perfectly, please go on.'

'. . . and you sent me a letter . . .'

A hushed voice: 'It is rather difficult to say anything at this juncture. Can you call me back in half an hour please?'

He'll be lucky. I wait a whole 60 minutes. His voice is entirely different, warm and friendly: 'I really am sorry. Simply could not speak when you rang. Work and colleagues, you know. Delighted you phoned, when can we meet?'

We fix up for lunch the next day. Meanwhile I spend some

time deciding what to wear for Hubert the crackshot. Nothing underneath, I think, although I'll keep my bra on.

I have butterflies buzzing around inside me. What will he be like, his face, the rest of him? I feel I am going to regret this.

The intercom squawks: 'I'm coming down.'

I feel ridiculous and snort in amusement. What the hell am I doing here waiting for a 10-inch prick? What do I want with a three-legged monstrosity? I can still take to my heels, stroll along the Boulevard Saint-Germain, window shopping, killing time. Oh Lord, here he is!

Hubert may not be all that tall, but he is certainly the tough type. Brown hair cut short, a not unpleasant twist to his smile, and the gaze of a man who can sum up a situation pronto. He plants a quick kiss on my lips, and I think that's honest.

'I imagined you taller.'

'I'm so sorry . . .'

'But I'm not at all disappointed.' (Flattery could save your life, Galia.)

He steps back to take a general view of yours truly. He scans me from tip to toe and back again.

'I've got good teeth,' I declare, opening my mouth wide.

'We're going to be friends, come on let's go up, you first.'

The staircase is narrow and we get to the first floor. I feel his hand on my bottom, evaluating the merchandise. 'Fine, fine,' he murmurs. I have an idea he has done this kind of thing before.

His apartment is so spick and span, I'm astonished. Low style furniture, brown painted walls, halogen lamps picking out three impressive abstract paintings. This cowboy has savvy.

'Did you do the decoration?' I ask nicely.

I hear a rumble that tells me nothing. Evidently it's not the matter uppermost in his mind. He says: 'Want a drink now or afterwards?'

Afterwards! The guy runs a tennis court, a golf course, a

fuck-o-rama, for pity's sake. I've got to slow him down.

'I'd like it now – the drink, I mean.'

'Scotch?'

'Something with less kick maybe?'

'Apple juice.'

'Fine.'

The strong silent type, I can see. I watch him pour out the juice, serve himself three fingers of the hard stuff, and raise his glass with a wink.

'To love!' he says. (This man could rip me apart, he's so direct.)

'To love! By the way, what does it mean for you, love?'

'I'm going to show you.'

'Oh good.'

He starts undressing, laying his things out on a chair: 'What's your name?' How many others has he had today?

'Galia, I told you.'

'Funny name.'

I unbutton my blouse, unsnap my bra, let my skirt fall. We are both as nature intended us and he scrutinizes me with an expert eye.

'Excellent, excellent.'

'What's excellent?'

'Everything. Shapely hips, tight arse, good bosom but on the small side, smooth skin, astonishing eyes. Excellent.'

My turn to give him the once over: 'Not bad yourself. Sturdy body, straight legs, well-contoured face, firm mouth but a little on the thin side. But tell me, that periscope of yours, you offered an outsize version, but it looks pretty standard to me. Could you have oversold it a little?'

'I said, when deployed.'

'Ah yes, deployed.'

'Suck it,' he commanded.

'I beg your pardon.'

'Suck.'

Orders are orders, and I initiate deployment. I kneel down and place his stick of toffee between my lips, holding on to

71

his buttocks for safety. His penis swells instantly like a balloon, but I swear I didn't blow! Within seconds his cock becomes dilated, only a third of it is in my mouth. I take a breather and stare at it.

'What a weapon!' My admiration was genuine, I can't believe it.

'Told you, didn't I?'

'Hold it a minute.' (He does.) 'Have you got a tape measure or something?'

'Go ahead, measure away.'

He hands me a ruler, I apply it along the workpiece, I read nine and a half inches and tell him. He won't accept it.

'Make sure you measure from the base, otherwise you lose at least half an inch. Measure along the underside, not the top.'

I keep to the topside and adjust the ruler: 10 inches precisely!

I shrug: 'Alright, you win. That's some decoration you have there.'

'And I know how to use it!'

We dive for the bed like champion swimmers. I have to admit, this pistolero is the best shot in the West. His whole middle torso pumps massively back and forth like a steam locomotive, tough luck for any cows on the line – redskins run for your lives! Three whistles and it's all over, and with minimum lubrication. I feel as if a hot poker scalded me inside. Hubert the Great rolls over on his back, sets fire to a cigarette and blows smoke rings. He has one arm under his head.

I cup my wounded sex and wait. At last he spits out: 'Well, how was it?'

'I figure you're a real big-shot,' I tell him.

II
FRENZY

May 25

Osvaldo and I let our hair down, but we do not tear it out. I lead him round to the idea that I need to keep my independence, that I cannot go on living full-time with him, that we shall go on meeting nevertheless.

Laurence B. has a studio free because she is getting married. This will be my place from now on.

Quite a few of my girl friends are finding husbands, and I am un-finding one. Who is right? There is no golden rule about this, and every girl must paddle her own canoe, as she can and wants. They chose a husband, I chose freedom. God helps those who help themselves.

May 26

I have time to jot down the extraordinary episode with the psychiatrist. 'I am physically in excellent shape, passionate and enthralling,' he had promised. He certainly has imagination.

For our lunch date he asked me to come to his office, where I learned he was finishing with the last of his morning patients. I waited in a small room the colour of porridge. There were three plastic chairs and a table with a dozen or so cigarette burns and loaded with a mass of dog-eared magazines. They were filthy, and the sight of them was enough to depress any patient. An empty waiting room with *ennui* running down the walls.

At length the 'likeable and easy to get on with' lady-killer appears in the doorway, a little 33-year-old man aged at least 40 in a dark blue three-piece suit. He has a large pallid head, big nose and thick glasses hiding a pair of tiny inquisitive eyes. I gulped at first sight; so this was God's gift to adolescent girls! I decided to play the innocent shy teenager, to give him confidence. The stark truth was that the man revolted me, but I reserved my judgement.

'Hullo, Dr Noroit.'

'How are you?' he says. 'You are much prettier than I imagined you. Come into my office.'

Old books, old armchairs, an old couch, everything old and dusty. Death cannot be far away. A ball of genuine anguish forms just above my navel.

He plops down in the chair behind his desk and studies me pensively, especially my bosom. I breathe in deeply and it rises.

'Everything alright, Galia?'

'Oh yes, I'm fine.'

A further silence. I love to see this disgusting creature wondering how to 'make' me, with his grey drooping head, his small searching eyes, his creepy surroundings. It is claustrophobic.

'So you're alright?' Does he always start like this?

I sum up the discussion so far: 'I am ALRIGHT!'

'Ah.'

He doesn't know which way to take me. It would be so much easier professionally if the patient would just spill out her story, he is thinking. Something like: 'Oh doctor, I simply don't know what's happening to me... I can't face life... I feel nobody cares for me...' etc. etc. He could then tell me to get on the couch and he could go ahead. But I refuse to bewail my lot.

Subsequent to a further silence, he ventures: 'Yes, you are extremely pretty. Tell me about yourself. We'll examine the problem together, shall we?'

'I don't feel like telling you about myself.'

'Indeed, why is that?'

'That's the way it is.'

He frowns and the big lenses take on a neurotic look. He is wondering how he can get me onto the couch, but he is shy.

Then my new Romeo blurts out in a quick mumble: 'I want to lie down with you Galia, you are, you are...'

Overcome, he removes his glasses, wipes them, scratches his nose, replaces his glasses, rubs his hands together and swiftly crosses his legs, banging a foot against the desk. He laughs like a schoolboy and declares: 'Well, I've said it, I want you, you are so... And your eyes are so exciting, so are your legs.'

I pull down my skirt but it won't cover my knees. I continue pretending I am innocent, stare at him as cruelly as I can, saying nothing. He slobbers on: 'Girls, I mean women, like you, and you really are a woman, there are so many. When I saw your advertisement I did not think, I mean I expected something else, someone less attractive if you see what I mean. You never know with advertisements. Last time, a while ago of course, she was quite awful, and you are so... I really did not expect a morsel, a woman like you. Ah Galia, Galia!'

Whereupon he throws himself at my feet, begins fondling my knees and hurting me as he squeezes them: 'Come on, let's make love, I want to so badly, I want to so badly...'

I clench my knees together and push his hands away, get up and scold him: 'How dare you doctor! You ought to be ashamed. Do you do this to all your patients?'

He kind of crumples and grovels as if I am going to smack

him: 'I'm sorry, forgive me, please forgive me . . .' He falls on
his face and whines, licking my shoes straps.

'Let me kiss your feet, I beseech you.' He kisses a shoe: 'I
want you, I want you, I want you!' The shoe is wet, he is
cringing, he is harmless after all, I decide to play him along.

His mouth sneaks up my leg, and I cry: 'Behave yourself,
doctor!' It only excites him more.

'Galia, Galia, oh please I must.' Frantically he unbuttons
his trouser front, feeling himself.

'No I'm sorry, you really aren't my type. Your letter was
nice, quite promising, but you are different somehow. It's no
go, I have to leave.

'Wait, oh wait.'

Panic seizes him, he leaps between me and the door, his
little acorn poking out, an awful grey colour. His glasses are
askew and he rivets his eyes on my skirt hem.

'Let me leave, please.'

'No, no, no!'

'If you don't let me leave, I shall scream. The whole
building will hear. I can scream really loud, your reputation
will be in shreds.'

He is rubbing his thing fast and whispering urgently: 'Just
wait two minutes, my little Galia, don't be beastly, your
knees . . .'

'Play with yourself as much as you like but don't you dare
come near me.'

His eyes are glistening: 'No I won't, I just want you to
watch me, yes watch me. Look Mummy! Oh it's coming,
Mummy, Mummy!'

As a measure of elementary precaution I take a step back,
but when he ejaculates it only goes a few inches, dripping
onto the carpet in short spurts.

Dr Noroit gasps and goes limp. He is wanked out, and he
collapses onto a chair where he straightens his glasses and
shamefacedly buttons up his trousers.

'Excuse me, Galia.'

'Think nothing of it, Yves. We all have our quirks. Now let

78

me go. Glad to have helped a little, better luck with the next ad.'

Outside, a warm bright sun makes it almost summer. The birds are chirruping away and people are thinking it's good to be alive. I take a deep breath and another and another.

Physically in excellent shape, passionate and tender at times. That's what the man said.

Not for the first time I realize how words can deceive, when you hear them, and even more when they are on a thin sheet of paper.

May 27

The more men I go with, the more questions I am asking myself about myself. I seem to be seeking vengeance in some way, and there is a kind of struggle for power between us.

I try to make myself indispensable to the male, like to see him needing me, I lure him – and immediately put a collar round his neck. I run along with my doggie on the leash, until I lose interest and look for another doggie.

Today I feel very feminine. I am scampering all over the place in search of the Ideal Man. He must be hero, sage, saint and perfect lover.

The ones I am meeting leave me crestfallen, and I suppose I try to obtain my revenge on these poor drips. I cannot find my Ideal Man. Meanwhile letters replying to my ad come pouring in. Whether the Dream Man is or is not in one of the envelopes, I decide to let them all out.

One of the suitors cannot spell, but that is not the aspect that worries me most.

Mademoisell,
Having read your letter and found it interesting, I have
decyded to reply. Let me introduce myself. I am 24,
imployed in an ofice, I am rather gay, stand six foot tall,
people say I am presentible, my leasure taste are simple,
cinema and modern music. Hopping you will reply to my

*adress which is France Remann, 12 rue de
Ménilmontant, Paris 75011.*

Sorry, Frankie boy, you make a curious prince charming.
There is a postcard from Istanbul showing the sunset over
the Bosphorus.

I am a French teacher in an Istanbul lycée *aged 32. I
love life or at all events I think I like what deserves to be
liked (what does* that *mean?) I cannot visit France as we
are allowed to quit Turkey once in three years. I invite
you to Istanbul where I live on my own, where I can put
you up easily. We can travel around, particularly along
the Aegean coast.*

Next, a letter in miniscule, regular, vertical script that I
can hardly see.

*I am 23 and in search of adventure and fun with
someone who is neither a submissive envious person or a
shrew who constantly shows me how wrong I am.
I am not a hearty male, but am convinced I am on the right
path. I offer all my resources to someone worthwhile, if I can
find her.
Can we work something out? Please reply, it might be worth
the try.*
Patrick *(address supplied)*

Another letter, written by a spider, it would seem.

*Mademoiselle,
This train is rocking along, but I hope you can decipher
these lines.
I am an engineer aged 35. I do not think I am an old fogey,
but that is a matter for you to decide at our first encounter,
and I hope you will write back.*

80

I could be the companion you are looking for! Awaiting
a word from you. Best Wishes.
Pierre
(Zig-zag signature, poetic and wild)

Next gentleman please!

Dear Mademoiselle,
I am a new man who would like . . .
(Photo enclosed – No!)
Greetings beautiful Unknown,
In the garden of my heart lies . . .

Next please!!

Now I am looking at the photo of a killer with a mustache, cauliflower ears and eyes like steel shafts.

Mademoiselle,
In response to your advertisement, yap yap yap . . . I shall
arrive at Saint Lazare station at 1952 hrs and stay at a
hotel in Rue Campagne 1er, Montparnasse. The enclosed
photo will enable you to recognise me and approach.
I arrive Sunday Saint Lazare 1952, or Tuesday same time
same place . . .

Press on.

Unknown Miss 853 6 A,
I am neither joker, nor fogey, nor has-been. I will not
claim to be good-looking, intelligent or rich or cultivated
or the rest of it. That is for you to judge.
You can leave a message on my answering machine, tel:
633.75.82. The timbre of my voice should give you some
idea of what lies behind it. If you do not like it, just hang
up, otherwise say where we can meet.
See you soon perhaps.
Emmanuel R.

With the rompings of the erotic film *Emmanuelle* foremost in my mind, I dial Emmanuel's number. The recorded voice I hear appeals to me, a lot. The diction is clear, the tone warm and a tiny bit nonchalant, lazy. I tell him: 'Phone me back as soon as you can, Galia.' I give my number.

He called me this evening, and we are seeing each other tomorrow at his place.

May 28
I think I am falling in love.

May 29
I met Emmanuel today.

The instant I set eyes on him, I knew that something important was about to happen to me.

He lives in a villa in the 14th *arrondissement*. The house is set back from railings as in an old provincial town, and you reach the front door past a flower-filled garden and a neatly-mown lawn. When I got there I found a man in a straw hat trimming the hedge. He has his back to me, of course, and I advance towards him stealthily.

'Hullo Emmanuel.'

He does not look around, and continues cutting away, delicately nipping the twigs.

'Huh, some welcome, I must say!'

He keeps on clip-clipping, and frankly I don't know what on earth to do. What kind of game is he playing? I stay where I am for about a minute, and then make a third attempt.

'Oh well alright, nice to have met you.'

Still no reaction. The fellow just keeps working on his silly hedge. He goes round a group of rose bushes, and suddenly he sees me. He is an old chap with blue eyes and a white mustache. He is clearly surprised. He is also as deaf as a poker.

'Hullo Mademoiselle, looking for someone?'

I take a big breath and yell: 'Emmanuel, it's me, Galia!'

'Of course, of course, Monsieur Emmanuel is behind there, I'll take you round.'

He has the deliberate stride of the gardener, and I fall in beside him as we crunch our way along a narrow gravel path round to the back of the house, which is facing south. My high heels are taking a beating.

A pleasant *terrasse* with lots of flowers. Some apple trees, cherry trees and a pear tree growing on trellis. It is hard to believe this is part of Paris, it's incredible, all that's missing is a cow and a few sheep. A friend who flew over the capital in a helicopter once told me the city is honeycombed with little gardens, old backyards, trees and blossoms. I am quite carried away; how lovely to live here in this enchanting villa.

The scrump-scrump of our footsteps reaches a man in a deckchair. He sees us at the very instant I am toppling sideways on my heels, he jumps up briskly, laying down a book. He moves languidly towards me.

The effect he has on me is startling. He is very good-looking, strikingly handsome and tall.

A curl of black hair curves down untamed, though with a certain elegance, over a finely-structured face. A pair of deep blue eyes are holding my gaze, honest eyes. Emmanuel is exactly like his voice, and I can feel the flush rising in my neck. We shake hands.

'Do sit down, Galia. I'm so glad you could come. What would you like to drink?'

I am mesmerized and I want to say 'you'. I force myself to keep still as I contemplate this superb male. How easy his movements, how naturally he converses. I cannot take my eyes off him, he gestures like a god, and his voice is heavenly music. This must be love, I tell myself, and I want to sob with joy.

'A beer perhaps, whisky, gin and orange?'

'Er-yes,' I manage to peep.

'But you haven't said. Fruit juice, then?'

'Yes please, fruit juice would be lovely.'

I lean forward in my chair, and he sits down on another next to me with the drinks. For the first time I am aware of his aroma. Every man has his aroma; it may be a strong smell or slight, sometimes animal, sometimes unpleasant or even ridiculous.

Emmanuel smells of cornfields, a bronzed body in the sun, a healthy body. A surge of desire courses through me and I am sure it shows.

'Why did you advertise, Galia?' he is saying. 'Surely an attractive woman like you finds no trouble meeting people...'

'I – I don't know really. I wanted the Unknown, I think.'

'Unknown people?'

'No, the Unknown – capital U. To broaden the scope...'

For a minute or so I chatter on about the Unknown, new experiences, Otherness. And I realize with horror that he does not seem to be interested. I have lost him already! At that instant I feel an overpowering urge to throw myself into his arms, tell him I am talking nonsense and no longer want to seek fresh fields, want to stay with him, forever.

'Emmanuel.'

'Yes?'

'I'd like to kiss you.'

Oh those eyes, as he turns to face me squarely: 'We mustn't rush things.'

And that's *you* in your place, silly bitch! Mortified, I can think of nothing to say. My throat thickens and I follow the tears as they well up. One escapes, trickles down my cheek. I feel a complete idiot.

'Please don't take it badly, Galia,' he counsels. 'I am simply asking you not to rush things between us. These "things" will happen or they won't. Let them take their course, and let's meet again soon. I'll phone you on Thursday, I promise.'

Thursday May 31
From break of day I stayed within inches of the phone. When it rang I jumped a yard. 'It's him!'. But it wasn't. Another candidate whom I cut short.

The temptation to phone him is driving me mad. I long to hear him just say a few words, to tell him I'm coming over right away. Let things take their course. It's easy for him!

Thursday 5 p.m.
Still no call.

Thursday 8 p.m.
I can't stand this any more. I am making a fool of myself.

Thursday 10 p.m.
Nothing, nothing, nothing. He hasn't rung me, hasn't kept his promise. He doesn't care, that's obvious. I am writing this just to try and reduce the tension, for something to do, something that helps take the pain away.

I even rang him 15 minutes ago, but no answer. He's probably laughing his head off. I just cannot sit still. A whole morning, noon and night waiting for that damn phone to ring. I've had enough, I am going out.

Friday June 1
At 10 a.m. this morning he called me.

'I tried to get you last night fairly late, but you were out. How are you?'

(How am I? I am like a mad thing. Mad over you, mad at you! Oh you wicked sod! My eyes are smarting but I am going to keep my dignity, we are both intelligent people, oh yes indeed!)

'I'm fine,' I say. It came out wrong.

'I was simply too busy earlier this morning...'

'Emmanuel!'

'Yes?'

'Oh nothing.'

'Yes, say it.'

'I would – would like to see you.'

'Good, let's have dinner. Let me see, next week, mid-week, how about that?'

My whole body seems to collapse. How about next week, he says. I can't believe he is saying that, I want it to be now in the next hour. Next week next year sometime never – how about that!

'Hullo, hullo, Galia, you still there?'

'Yes, I'm still here.' Speechless, however, dripping like a wet rag.

'You seem strange, anything the matter?'

Oh no, there's nothing the matter with me. I just want to die that's all, creep under the carpet and die.

'Emmanuel, I want to tell you...'

'Yes?'

'Oh nothing. Next week, then.'

I replace the receiver, and hurl myself at my bed, shrieking in agony, buckets of tears soaking into the pillow, my legs kicking in frustration.

I am not a weeper by nature, but this time I cannot help it.

June 8

It is all over with Emmanuel, before it ever started.

With him I was completely gaga, it was genuine and it was the first time for me. It just wasn't the same for him.

Never before had (have) I been so in love with a man, and he turned out to be the most inaccessible of them all. Maybe it was simply bad luck; all I know is that he never did unbend with me. He found he 'respected' me, I was 'intelligent' and 'highly attractive'. But it went no further. He did not even

86

bother to explain his reservations, did not come clean about them.

I realize there is no point in hurting myself day after day. He probably found me amusing. I am too proud, I don't know.

My beautiful love story had no beginning and no end. My entire existence was transformed overnight, and it disappeared in a puff of smoke.

But life goes on, I won't turn the knife in the wound. I will simply have to forget the episode if I can.

June 12

I badly needed a change of outlook, and I picked out the most jovial-sounding applicant.

I rang him and went to see him on the seventh floor of the old block in Les Halles, the former Paris central markets.

He is a smallish chap with curly blond hair, rather sweet and full of fun. He says he is 33 but looks 10 years younger. It makes a change.

'Poor Galia, you look as though the world's come to an end,' he chuckled rather nicely when he let me in. 'Come on, let's drown our sorrows in a Meurseault '49. Can't get much of it these days. I found it at Fauchon's, it's an offer you can't refuse. Hah!' He fetched a carton of supermarket biscuits.

He went babbling on and it was good for me: 'You know the Chinese Wheelbarrow? I'll show you later. I'd love to play Chinese Wheelbarrows with you. And the Monkey Up A Tree, you know that? I'll show it to you. And there's the Wild Geese Flying Upside Down, doesn't ring a bell? You're so innocent, a little kitten fallen out of the nest.'

'Cat's don't live in nests.' This man is crackers!

'How do you know? I have read Kant, Schopenhauer and Kierkegaard, and none of them deny that cats can live in trees, and can fly. I see plenty of them flying about at night between this window and the tower of Saint Eustache over there. They are asleep now, of course, trying to digest their

87

gloppy food in tins; drugs, that's what those catfoods are. All cats are mortal. Socrates is mortal, *ergo* Socrates is a cat. And here he is, Socrates, my dozy cat!'

I broke in: 'And what's your own name? You haven't told me.'

'Hey, you're a fast worker. I'm not telling you my innermost secrets in the first two minutes, one has one's self-respect.'

Falling in with his flippancy, I say: 'What's the Monkey Up A Tree, and the Geese Flying Upside Down?'

'Those are two classic Chinese positions. In one, we are face to face – don't worry I'll show you – and in the other the woman stretches out on the man and she faces upwards. The whole art of it depends on the way the male, that's me, makes his thrusts during coitus.'

'Coitus!'

'Coitus. Alternate deep and slight penetrations, by magic numbers: 5 deep, 8 slight. You do it on the floor, and some mystical schools of thought say the male should not ejaculate. But on this aspect of the theory, I am a complete dissident. In any case I have no choice. What do you think of my Meurseault?'

'It's super.'

'Cheap too.'

'But tell me, I may not be too keen on your Chinese physical jerks.'

'In that case I shall rape you, which involves us in an entirely different erotic pigeon-hole, more Western. I may even kill you, Western style and not with the refinement of the Chinese tradition: first an ear, then an eye, another ear, a foot, and so on. Slowly and surely. Westerners are so crude, they just shove a knife in and it's all over. Such decadence! What's your preference then?'

'The Orient. Give me lots of tiny deaths, Chinese style.'

Two hours later we are lying on our backs like a pair of pussycats after feeding time.

'I liked it, all those *chinoiseries*.'

'You've seen nothing yet,' he cried in a clipped nasal voice, making his eyes into slits with his fingers. 'We behaved like crude lubricious wild animals, shoddy china objects, instruments of utter decadence...'

'Eroticism certainly calls for inventiveness.'

'Everything has been invented already. The sum total of know-how is vast, it's in the National Libraries of Amorous Science. We feeble unrefined missionaries of the West are miles away from the beginnings of erotic science. The ancient Chinese, for example, had an extraordinary way of copulating, and it may still be going on.

'The man and the woman are seated face to face on the floor in the lotus position. They are in the nude, they gaze into each others' eyes, their eyes caress the other's body. And they wait. They are not allowed to touch, but they smell the breath and fragrance of the other, so that their desire mounts to dizzy heights. This goes on for some hours. They hardly know each other, they have never touched, they are deprived of love-making as we understand it. This, you will realize, is an explosive situation. It goes on and on, and the man's penis is like a ramrod for hour after hour, and the woman is steamy too but it doesn't show as much. Then suddenly the man is swept away by the whirlwind of orgasm. He is motionless, yet he ejaculates long hot streams onto the woman, and this triggers the woman's orgasm. After that she throws back her head and swoons. Sometimes she comes first, and this brings on her companion's orgasm.'

He paused and then continued: 'To attain this level of perfection, you need immense expertise, long training, the backing of an entire culture, century upon century of amorous science. So you can imagine the contempt I have for our sniggering compatriots in the bistros telling dirty jokes, recounting their sexual exploits and their next conquest. For 20 centuries Western sexuality has been hamstrung by the concept of sin, and our sexual culture dominated by what is prohibited. The result is that men and women and children and old folk are in a corner, bitter and peevish, trying constantly to extend the law that is written between every line of our loves: thou shalt not come.'

I give a sigh: 'Oh my Chinese Master, thou hast not revealed thy name.'

'My name is Tien Hang Tsu, which means...'

'Oh come on, tell me.'

'My name is Alphonse...'

'Stop that.'

'... and I bounce!'

'Please tell me your name.'

'My name, *femme fatale*, I will tell you. My name... Good heavens, is that the time? I shall have to move fast.'

I raise my voice a tone: 'You're not moving anywhere. I want your name or...'

'Or what?'

'I'll strangle you.'

'Oh transport of delight! Now I won't tell you anything because, my sweetie, strangulation is the *ne plus ultra* of paradisiac ejaculation. Quick, find a scarf.'

I try another tack: 'If you don't give me your name, I won't strangle you!'

'How superbly logical women are, she wants it both ways! Let's just get the strangling over, shall we? My name's Matthieu.'

'Matthieu?'

'Certainly, Matthieu. As in passion, short-arse, saint, boss of money-changers and usurers.' This nonsense was helping me so much, I started to giggle.

And then: 'Matthieu, it's a nice name.'

'Matthieu wants to be strangled nicely.'

And so we went on playing like children all afternoon, and I managed to forget my unrequited love. In this attic in the entrails of Paris I relived my lost exuberance. Perhaps it was doing him good too.

'Matthieu, teach me another Chinese caress. Please, Matthieu.'

'I'll demonstrate the Chinese Fish, if you like, but we need someone to tie our hands together.'

'Tie our hands!'

'The Chinese Fish method consists of Madam Yin and Mister Yang lying down naked and bound on a mattress to make love like fish do, without using their hands.'

'Sounds delicious, much better than Chinese nougat. I'm sure it's out of this world.'

'We'll do the Fish when we have someone who knows their knots. Lie down. Put your glass over there, I'm going to give you the Spring Butterfly. Close your eyes first, no don't cheat this is serious, now relax. You are next to a stream in the province of the Yang Tse. It is midday, your warrior has gone off to work, that is, to fight. Your servants are collecting grasshoppers for the soup and you are in the meadow in the sun among the flowers, naked as a water lily, a brightness in the mist. You are beautiful, you are dreaming of your glorious master and of his strong arms, his beautiful sword; and you are dreaming too of the young lord who lives across the way, of the smooth flesh of his thighs. Suddenly, a butterfly . . .'

For a long, incredible and marvellous hour, Matthieu makes his butterfly fly. With a very fine silk brush he strokes the most sensitive parts of my body, hidden parts I never knew about: behind my ears, in the bend of my wrist, the backs of my knees, between my toes. The sensations he accorded me were extraordinary, exquisite, tiny electric spasms on my skin. I begin to feel the subtle excitement coming on, I want the caresses to be firmer.

He knows this because he is diabolically clever, but he keeps me waiting. Matthieu takes a small bottle of the oil, yellow and perfumed, dips another silk brush a little larger in the oil, and unexpectedly stops everything.

'Matthieu,' I whisper, 'please go on, please . . .'

'The butterfly has flown to a branch, but it will return.'

'Matthieu, you are torturing me, let me get it off please, with you.'

'The butterfly is nudging the flower. We must be still and

91

wait. Ah, there it is on another bloom.'

Then he slowly opens my legs, spreads my own little flower with utmost care, lifts my clitoris with the brush and begins to caress it upwards with the end of the oily brush, and then round and round and round. The pleasure this affords me is unbelievably intense, I am excruciatingly exposed. I am panting as I whisper in a high voice: 'Yes, oh yes, more more, please Matthieu.'

At that instant Matthieu covers me with his body, and I feel him enter me. But we do not move, time stands still, and together our orgasms, our united orgasm, bursts forth in a climactic symphony.

June 15

I cannot help thinking of Emmanuel, and I feel quite dreadful. I am trying to pretend the pain is not there by plunging into a round of activity: I go shopping, clean my windows, tidy the kitchen cupboards – anything to stop the aching obsession with Emmanuel, this impossible love story.

The worst time is around three in the morning, when I have a knife entering my very heart, reminding me of my lost Emmanuel. Hell must be like this. In the still of the night I lie in my bed with my eyes wide open to see his eyes, his hands, his hair, his smile. It hurts terribly.

I cannot weep, I cannot sleep, and I hopelessly resort to Valium and barbiturates. I can't stand the suffering, am afraid of the pain. Sleep becomes a nightly suicide enabling me to keep going for another day.

June 16

Mummy phoned. Daddy has been taken to hospital with a heart attack, but his life is not in danger, she tells me.

The news leaves me indifferent, and all I am concerned about is how she is taking it. I am not ashamed of this daughterly callousness, for I never loved my father. I hated him for not making Mummy happy and still do. He is a stranger for me now and his death would not affect me. I am an ungrateful daughter but that is the way it is, one cannot fabricate love. Even so, I get Interflora to send a bouquet of lilies, though my heart is not in it.

I am unconditionally and fervently tender towards the mother I love. But the time she has herself lost in mediocre love will never come back. My father did not deserve this sublime woman.

June 17

Elisabeth R. sent me some junk mail announcing the opening of a 'College for Women' near the Arc de Triomphe. She describes it pompously as 'a higher institute of erotological research'. To please her I pay the subscription.

It transpires that a former street-walker from Rue Saint Denis, who first tried running a bar in the 5th *arrondissement*, had the idea of a training centre for prostitutes. Later the project evolved and took in some students from Censier faculty.

Together these students set up the College for Women, rather as a joke but also as a challenge and an intellectual game. Its aim is to teach eroticism to women. Madame De Chaussoy, the ex-street-walker's assumed name, apparently takes the venture very seriously. This is no lighthearted enterprise but a genuine school for women in the sexual desert who want to learn the skills of lovemaking. The women who are prepared to pay for this instruction include girl students, housewives, society women, the elderly, young people – all sorts.

Today was the first day of the first term, and the Directress as she calls herself delivered an inaugural address. She is a buxom blonde of nearly six foot, outrageously made up, an Olympic weight-putter by the look of her.

The lecture hall in Avenue Niel is fairly small, and the students (all women of course) took their seats rather timidly under the severe scrutiny of Madame De Chaussoy. The average age seems to be about 40, a time of life when women have the urge to make up for lost time – while there is still time! There are a few girls a wee bit older than I am, but yours truly is the baby of the class. Some of the oldsters keep glancing at me: they give off hostility, admiration, hatred, perhaps desire in some cases. How unfair to be young, they seem to be telling me. But I would like to stare back and tell them: 'I'll be old one day too.'

Madame De Chaussoy calls for silence, which is unnecessary since nobody has breathed a word since we came in.

'Mesdames, Mesdemoiselles,' she declares. 'This is neither a whore-house, nor Women's Lib nor a university establishment. You have come to the College for Women to learn what you have never learned so far: to be a woman. You went to school but they did not teach you what was essential. The universities taught you abstractions, Women's Lib teaches you hostility, the whore-house taught you submissiveness!' Mumbling breaks out in the hall. 'Yes I know you haven't come out of whore-houses, but it's the same thing: you have lived under conjugal fealty for centuries with men crushing you with their power. The reaction of Women's Lib to this defeat has been "Get rid of men and let's live on our own." But you know very well ladies that this is not possible, there is no such thing as a happy homosexual.' Slight mumbling from parts of the hall.

'Man and Woman, male and female, are two complementary forces. Without their encounter there can be no true enjoyment.

'The toughies of Women's Lib suggest you eliminate Man. I propose to you that you find Man again, and win him over.' A pause. The speaker takes a few deep breaths into her mighty chest, scanning the gathering with ferocious eyes.

She continues: 'We love men, we do!' Applause. 'But subjection we shall not admit.' Applause. 'We too have the right to power.' Applause. 'And this power we shall win through men's orgasms!'

Another silence, in case we have not understood. A cloud of uncertainty and doubt floats above our heads.

The Directress breaths again and booms out: 'We have got them by their weak points, ladies.' Prolonged applause at this and stamping of high heels. 'Silence please. Thank you. Jesus said he would teach us virtue, but God is dead. Nietzsche showed us Superman, Freud showed us the Subconscious, Marx declared "workers of all lands unite". The workers united and with barbed wire inside and all around we can see what that has produced. We see that, Subconscious or no Subconscious, people are still in the doghouse and so are their psychoanalysts. As to the Supermen, we have watched them marching in their tin hats and jackboots within living memory.

'But I say to you that I will teach you the pleasure, the reconciliation and the knowledge that comes with love. I will give you neither paradise nor glory, but you will feel better in your women's bodies.'

This afternoon we had Practical, using a rubber man. He was a full-scale painted latex doll with two detachable penises: one limp, one erect. The pricks are unscrewed like hot water bottle stoppers and you work on one or the other depending on the stage of your instruction, while a smiling paratrooper head looks down on the flabby body.

The first lesson was the limp penis. We were asked: 'Your man has come home from work, he is tired and lies down on the bed. You want to make him want sex. What do you do?'

A volunteer is called for. Claudine, a petite brunette from somewhere round Marseilles, says she will have a go. Smiling broadly she approaches the paratrooper, hesitates and then gives him a quick kiss on the lips. She doesn't seem too convinced about it and looks round at us with a sheepish smile. Claudine then grabs hold of the rubber prick, it wobbles about but she manages to pump it up and down, fairly energetically.

Madame De Chaussoy intervenes: 'You're being too

rough, Claudine, in too much of a hurry, you're shaking him like a baby's bottle before he has time to think about it. Softly, sensually. Next!'

Madame has scared everyone off already, but as no-one else volunteers I say I will have a shot at the paratrooper.

'Fine Galia, show us how you do it.'

I move up to the kind of operating table where the male object lies waiting, and pull him round a bit, then put the rubber cylinder in my mouth.

I hope Claudine doesn't have anything catching, although anything is better than syphilis. The prick is all ploppy and yukky and cold, and the man's thighs have that soapy rubber smell. But the insides are slippery too and I feel a little itch beginning inside me. It's sort of naughty. I can see why sex-starved men buy inflatable dolls, especially if the dolls' eyelids flutter. Rubber is nice to handle and my own fantasies start moving in as I speed up.

'Not too bad, Galia,' I am informed. 'But please, ladies, do not forget the object of the exercise. What would you think if your companion immediately started chomping at you? ('He's never chomped at me,' I hear a woman muttering behind me. 'Wouldn't mind it if he did now and again.') Delicately, ladies, fastidiously, like this; I just run my fingers over the whole body, upwards of course, never stopping, never pressing. Very light quick touches along the thighs, arms and chest. Then I move in with a quick flip to the penis, and away again. He is beginning to come alive now. So please remember: Phase I, lightness of touch.

'Phase II, still light, but focusing on the organ with tiny licks using the end of your tongue, like a feather on this side then upwards and ABOVE ALL no oral insertion yet. Let's not run before we leap. Our man is now excited and his work and worries and fatigue are far behind him. He wants sex, so . . .' (She unscrews the limp prick which is now wet, puts it on a shelf under the table, screws on the biggie. The paratrooper is looking more interesting now.) 'More licks, not too fast there's plenty of time, languidly, while you continue feathering your hands all over the body.

'Phase III: alternate licking and insertion. Six licks, and in, six licks and in, 10 or 15 cycles. Our man is now jumping for joy. Ladies, you have him just where you want him!'

She adds mundanely: 'That's all for today. Tomorrow nine o'clock for sexuality in the Trobriand Islands.'

June 18

At the College I have made a friend of Myriam. She is 28, a little on the chubby side, but a stupendous blonde. She is finishing psychology and starting at the Louvre. She is a strange girl, highly independent and bursting with energy. She writes serial love stories for a magazine.

She confides to me that she acts like a man in many ways. It is she who chases men, manipulates them, makes use of them and then discards them. She can't get enough of sex, she says.

'Come along,' she said when we emerged into Avenue Niel today, 'Let's pick up a man for ourselves. Why shouldn't women take the initiative?'

Close by the Arc de Triomphe, Myriam scans the male talent and picks out a nice little chap about to enter the Metro station. She falls in behind, tugging me along.

'He's real cute, don't you think?'

The man stops and turns, visibly astonished.

'Nice, eh, Galia? A juicy piece, I'd say. Yes I mean you, sweetie.' The fellow turns as red as a beetroot, and she goes on: 'Don't be afraid, handsome, I like your eyes! D'you live with your parents? Oh Galia, take a load of that bottom, beautiful, my word I could go for that.'

The poor man looks terrified, as she persists: 'What's your name, Charlie? Lost your tongue? Sulking?'

Myriam moves in and plants a kiss on his mouth. He mumbles 'But, but' and she says: 'There is no but about it. Oh come on, we don't mean any harm, we just want a bit of fun, give us a kiss. Hurry up, round here.' She pushes him against

97

a tree, where he looks ready to be executed. I am definitely roused, if it's as easy as this. 'You first, Galia.'

I hoist my little self onto the tips of my toes and kiss him nimbly. I detect a fleeting interest from him. Myriam says: 'That's more like an accolade, my turn now.' She gathers the man and the tree in a single swoop, somehow manages to open his mouth and twirls her tongue round inside, simultaneously undoing his belt regardless of passers-by. Her hand slithers down his trouser front, and the man closes his eyes. He likes it!

Still smooching, she gropes him for a couple of minutes and stands back with spittle running down her chin. She is flushed and lets him escape.

As we walk away she says in my ear: 'I went right round to the rear entrance.' Myriam is certainly over-sexed.

June 19

Dinner with Osvaldo. He is in love with a girl just over 18. Eighteen is the lower limit under law, and he is scared of the law. She is a smallish student from Quebec with rosy cheeks and that amazing French Canadian accent. He seems keen on Emilie, but I know already that he likes adolescents.

'Do you know what the Canadians say when anyone gets irritated?'

'No.'

'They say "Don't climb up the curtains". And d'you know what she calls a mint-lemonade? "Fast lawn water juice". You must meet her, she is delightful.'

I am genuinely pleased for Osvaldo. All's well that ends well. Things are never as bad as they seems. Life goes on. Dear Osvaldo!

June 20

I have had a rollicking from my sisters. They say I should have gone with them to see father at Tours. I let them prattle on, I cannot be bothered to argue back.

I am in another world, the only real family tie I have is with Mummy. I simply cannot raise any interest in the others. I must be quite monstrous, morally speaking, but at least I do not pretend to be a little angel.

Even if it is hard going at times, I shall never give in and conform. If my four sisters want to continue the tradition of respectability, that is their affair.

I find life is too momentous a thing, too exhilarating to waste in a standard mould.

Instinctively I believe I am right to be a wildcat. Whatever they think, I have learned more than they ever got from their fancy education.

June 21, first day of summer

Myriam and I feel on top of the world as we trip down Avenue Niel with arms linked in our gaily-swinging 1920s' above-the-knee dresses.

When Myriam perceives a male she likes the look of, she gives him a whistle without stopping to see the effect. I am drawn to her but she is quite a phenomenon and I still haven't worked her out. Today I asked her: 'Do you sometimes meet a man you like and take him home?'

'Naturally.'

'And you make love with him?'

'Sure, if I like him.'

'And keep on seeing him?'

'Not usually. When I've had what I want, it's bye-bye Johnny and no violins.'

'In fact you do like men do: have your poke and walk off.'

She laughs: 'Just like Don Juan without the talk. It's hullo, we go upstairs, I straddle him, we wash it off, cheers.'

'And that's enough for you?'

'It's fun while it lasts, but it's no worse than a man who sleeps all over town without love coming into it. Being in love is completely different.'

'Are you in love often?'

'Rarely. Men have always disappointed me. They are egotistical, always going on about their work, they take themselves too seriously, they don't give their whole selves. Life has turned them into liars and bluffers. And those who refuse to be young turks, greedy for power, end up drop-outs or merely bitter. That's the way men are today. Women are far more interesting, deeper, absorbing.'

Since she is prepared to talk, I go further: 'I find it hard to understand why a girl like you is at the College for Women. You are already fulfilling yourself. Do you just want to become more expert in lovemaking?'

'Hm, expert? I know perfectly well how a man likes it. I do it all the time. I'm at the College out of curiosity, for the enjoying of it, for the company almost. It's an amazing project, launched in the face of prudishness and hypocrisy. Mother De Chaussoy fought for months to open that College, and I felt she deserved backing.'

This morning our Directress was in a good mood. Her athlete's face was almost kind, transformed after 90 minutes of make-up.

'Ladies,' she said, 'I am very pleased with you. You have made great progress.' (Old Ma Chaussoy handing out compliments, whatever next?) 'You are not fully expert yet but you have grasped the elementary techniques. No man will resist you, I am sure.

'So far we have been working *in abstracto*, but from today we start *in vivo*. The models you will be experimenting on now are well and truly alive. Let me introduce you.'

Three lovely men then came in. A tall blond man, the elegant kind you see at the Racing Club de France; a squat stocky man with black hair, obviously highly virile; a slender, brown-haired, delicate looking man with a fine bone structure, almost effeminate.

The sound level rises as we start cooing like doves. The woman next to me bawls in my ear: 'Oh what a hunk of meat!' 'Which one?' 'On the right of course, who else?' She

100

means hairy.

De Chaussoy: 'I would like to present to you: Gérard, Hughes and Cyril.' The three bow nicely, scanning the women like Christians in the coliseum sizing up the lions.

Madame De Chaussoy certainly knows how to pick her stallions. The sportsman, the brute and the nice one. We all can't wait to ride them, but we want to see their livery first. *In vivo veritas!*

Perhaps they are going to do us a striptease. Or maybe go out and come in again naked. We all wriggle in our seats.

The Directress declaims: 'First we are going to see how a sensual woman undresses a man. I want someone for Cyril. Come now, ladies, don't be shy.'

Cyril is so long and thin he looks like a virgin being auctioned in a slave market. He lowers his eyes.

'Reckon he's a nancy boy?' Myriam says in a whisper everyone can hear.

'Of course not, Cho-Cho would never have picked a homo.'

Cho-Cho is getting impatient: 'Instead of yapping like a bunch of 15-year-olds, show a little initiative. Undressing a man isn't going to give you a baby!'

Old Sophie steps up. Actually she is only about 50, and still alluring.

'A volunteer for Hughes, please.'

'Me!' yells the woman next to me. And to make sure of her man she strides towards the dark guy and grabs his arm.

'Now, anyone for Gé...'

'Me, me, me, me!' A dozen voices screech out.

'Oh dear, ladies, let's not lose our reserve. Valentine, you take Gérard. Quiet please, we are not in the infants school. You will all get your turn. The three gentlemen on the platform please, and let's see how we get on. Ready? You can start now, I'm not telling you a thing at this stage.'

A hush falls on the hall as we watch the three heroes divested of their clothing, item by item, by their three females. Almost the Folies Bergère, it's so entertaining.

Gérard acts up, knowing how resplendent he is. Head high, he sticks out his chest when his shirt drops away.

Hughes looks like a chimpanzee in disguise, a bashful one at that, but he submits to his female, who just can't get him undressed fast enough.

Cyril still has his eyes on the floor; he lets Sophie go ahead, lifting his long arms so she can remove his pink T-shirt.

We are now approaching the moment of truth. Gérard and Hughes are in their underpants, but Cyril still has his shoes and trousers on. Sophie takes her time, her motions are unruffled and loaded with suggestiveness, her hands peeling off the garments lovingly. Sophie was born for this, we feel. But Cyril is clearly uncomfortable, there is a bump in there somewhere and we can all see it, and he knows we can see it. Amid a highly-charged silence his trousers fall, and a murmur of admiration flutters through the hall, for his thin turquoise slip is projecting out in front like the bow of an ocean liner. The atmosphere is distinctly clammy, you can smell it.

Cho-Cho starts up: 'Well, ladies, we are now at the nub of our problem. Need I say more? The evidence is before your eyes. Once again you will realize that haste does not pay. Sophie knew that. Right, gentlemen, get dressed and we'll try another three . . .'

The entire hall lets out a sigh. 'Oh!' Frustration looks like part of Cho-Cho's technique.

June 26

In my fireplace, the whole pile of the letters replying to the ad is waiting to go up in flames. I cannot really answer them all. I have met some of these men and, apart from Emmanuel I wish I had not, although I would not have lost out on Matthieu in Les Halles.

I have been offered all shapes and sizes, every imaginable colour of eyes, I have seen a good many white marks where a wedding ring has been hastily removed, some candidates have cheered me up and others have told me with a shudder that life is black except when I am there. Actually it is true that in the case of some, life had a taste of the sewer.

I came across professional copulators, men with obsessions, perverts, hystericals and psychopaths. And I am fed up with the whole damn lot of them. Every single letter is in the fireplace, I am a female Beelzebub.

June 28

A phone call from Jemal Abdelaziz Faraoud, Prince of Araby. He holds nothing against me, and I've nothing against him. He is staying at the Stella-Park Hotel on Avenue François 1er, which is reputedly the most expensive in the world.

He asks me to meet him this evening in the bar of the Stella. He will introduce me to some 'very important friends,' he says.

June 29

I must get this night at the Stella-Park down while I can.

Jemal welcomed me with open arms and introduced me to his friends: a Saudi businessman, an attaché at some Embassy, an American businessman and an Arab Minister of Technology or Transport, I forget which. I never had a chance to check because the moment we sat down everything started to go crazy.

The bar was crowded with about 100 billion dollars. Greying financiers out of a picture book, de luxe call girls, foreigners of all sorts, the Paris-based jet set in action.

My hosts are already fairly advanced with their drinking, whisky for Uncle Sam and champagne for the others. The Minister seemed to be most lucid, and from time to time his personal male secretary came up with a telex, which he scanned and then blew something in the ear of the secretary who would bow and disappear.

The conversation was in English except for a few asides in Arab. Probably dirty jokes.

Two girls join us, pretty little things used to hanging onto the world's richest testicles. All they needed was bunny ears and they could have come straight from Playboy. They were cheap, stupid and ravishing. For a moment I wished I had their brazen sex-appeal.

The blonde one was the more professional at first sight, and she immediately sat curvaceously on the Minister's lap. The other, not so striking in appearance, nestled cosily between the two thickest wallets in the group: Jemal ($1 million) and the American ($750,000), I would guess.

I watched the girls' gold-digger faces, their letter-box smiles. It looked like they had got themselves a fat retirement pension. I had to admire them.

We went into eat round a huge table. While the little bunnies swayed their bottoms on their chairs, the men talked of interest rates, women, capital cities, beaches and casinos. The Minister got up twice after glancing at some messages, but was soon back. Jemal, sitting next to me, confided in a low steady voice that he was most upset by my hasty departure from Cannes.

'I can't understand it, Galia, you left so hurriedly and so unfairly.'

'Forgive me, Jemal, I was in a dreadful crisis of emancipation, I was unable to stand the least constraint.' I gave him what I hoped was a sweet smile.

'But I did not impose constraints on you.' It was rather satisfying, after all, having this sheikh pleading with me.

'I really can't remember. I only *felt* restricted, in bonds. It was probably my fault rather than yours. I'm sorry I upset you.' I laid my hand lightly on his arm.

'Do not excuse yourself. You followed your impulses and you were quite right . . .'

One of the bunnies hiccupped over her champagne and broke in with a baby voice: 'No private sessions. Come and sit by me, Jemal.'

My ex-prince was embarrassed and threw me a hopeless glance. I worked my eyelashes to tell him: 'Go ahead and have fun, Jemal. Sure, she's an idiot, but we are not here to rake over the past, and we are still friends, you and I. In any case, she has lovely thighs, go and stroke them.'

By midnight we were all in the azure blue of the Stella swimming pool, with exotic green-leaved plants all around us. The two pink rabbits have nothing on, and their bodies are so superb it doesn't seem to matter how they get their money.

One of them is doing a slow underwater yankee-doodle-dandy on the American who is hooked with his arms to the pool edge, his bathing trunks around his knees. He looks like he is being crucified and is mouthing: 'Oh Gard, it's so good in the water, I didn't know it could be so great. My Gard!' Every 30 seconds the girl comes up for air and then plunges again. The more she sucks, the louder he blows.

The Minister goes back and forth doing the breast stroke. He is smiling and still sober. His secretary comes to the pool edge and shows him another telex, looking out of place in his suit and waistcoat.

I can see Jemal with the super-blonde in the foliage. She is leaning back with her wonderful legs gaping and he is licking her genitalia, his head nodding like an alsation dog. She makes quite a thing of her jerky little motions and is twiddling her toes just a little. She utters whimpering noises and is gasping, and I find it enthralling. She seems to be liking it and it may be genuine; this stirs my own concupiscence. I stealthily move close until I can see Jemal's tongue working repeatedly into her opening and then upwards again and again, sometimes darting into the crease in her bottom. Jemal has progressed a lot, I am jealous a bit.

The Embassy attaché is nowhere to be seen. I thought he looked a little sneaky and may be hiding in a cabin masturbating. The Saudi businessman has drunk bottle after bottle of champagne and keeps laughing.

A nice respectable orgy for the start of the 1980s, I am

thinking. But, although I feel the flesh motioning, I would rather not join in. I cannot honestly say why, this may be just an 'off' day for me. Even so, I won't spoil the others' fun and, when the party moves off towards the Minister's suite, I cheerfully tag along. The pink bunnies move through the hotel in beachrobes dripping with water. A guest comes out of the lift where we are waiting, a typical English duke or something, and with one accord the girls fling wide their robes, revealing everything. His eyes pop out of his head, and he will need a week to get over it. On the other hand, who knows, it may be the start of a whole new fantasy world for him. He must be at least 68. I would love to watch a duke playing with himself.

We get to the Ministerial suite, all of us except the attaché who is probably locked in his cabin. The suite measures 1500 square feet in all, I am told. It has five bedrooms, several balconies, a solarium, bullet-proof windows, electronic bug detectors, telephones and of course the telex, little palm-trees and other things in boxes, television and a video tape recorder, plus bathrooms fitted out with various sexually-inviting aids.

The Minister has about a ton of champagne sent up. At first a waiter in smart black attire came in with six bottles. Above the noise the Minister yells: 'Six bottles, you must be mad, I said lots of champagne, get six cases up here.'

They can say what they like about the Arabs, but they certainly know how to throw a party. The Minister and Jemal empty the six crates, and then empty the bottles – into the bath, where it bubbles. Corks are popping about all over the place, and the music is deafening.

The blonde bunny cannot resist the bubbles, and slides into the bath. The Minister starts splashing the champagne all over her, but the male secretary comes up with a telephone and his boss grabs it.

'Jeddah, Your Excellency.' Immediately after that: 'Los Angeles, Your Excellency.'

The Minister barks his orders down the phone as the

bunny squeals with delight and the rock rhythm makes the crystalware tinkle in unison. Thus are the affairs of the planet decided.

In due course I had to lie down in one of the bedrooms, overcome with champagne and noise. I fell asleep and missed the belly dancer. The party broke up around dawn.

July 1

Money trouble looms. I find I am unable to pay the rent and certain other bills.

I have no intention of taking to the streets. I could ask Mummy, and I know she would give her last sou for me, but I would not do that to her. She has pinched and scraped all her life for us children.

I make a few phone calls to friends. I am decidedly embarrassed about asking them.

Tomorrow I am 21, and wish I could be more cheerful about it.

July 2

Matthieu flings a birthday party for me in his attic. Myriam, Osvaldo, Jemal and Elisabeth are among the guests.

At one point in the evening I can hold back the tears no longer. I weep because I am just as stupid as I was two years ago, three years ago, five years ago.

As a little girl I used to tell myself: 'When I am grown-up I shall understand everything.' I am grown-up and I still don't understand a thing. I am less naive, and it simply makes life more difficult to cope with.

July 3

Today I was asked to play in a hard porn film, 4,000 francs for a week's work. It's not exactly a star's fee but I agree to do it. I am in dire financial straits and in any case it will be something different.

Filming is to take place from 6 p.m. to midnight, which means I shall not miss any lectures. That counts most.

July 4

I have now met the actors playing in *Charlotte Mouille Ta Culotte* (Charlotte Wet Your Panties).

It was Gérard, the dazzling model from the College for Women, who got me the job, and he is playing the principal role. He told me he had done seven porn films already; he is completely *blasé* about it and yearns to play in 'real' films as the star. One problem he has is his diction, but frankly he is also a terrible actor, stiff, melodramatic and unconvincing. Gérard has also done three serials for television, and the other star Nadia told me he definitely will not get any more T.V. work.

Nadia is a small blonde of 22 from Poland, rather on the plump side and with short legs, but she has magnificent green eyes.

I have the supporting woman's role. In fact there are just the three of us in the cast.

The story line could never win an Oscar in a thousand years. A man (Gérard) and his wife (Nadia) seduce a girl friend (me) who is staying with them, initiating her into the joys of triangular sex. And that's it! The producer came up with the understatement of the century when he murmured to me: 'With our budget, we can't really go in for creative work.'

'But why not?' say I in all innocence. The question shook him rigid, and for the rest of the evening I was the bright-eyed 'intellectual' of the party.

The film crew consists of a chief operator (he prefers to be known as the photo director for some reason), an assistant cameraman, a sound engineer, an electrician who seems half asleep most of the time, a continuity girl and of course the producer (he prefers 'director') whose word is law. The producer comes from the wilds of central France but he calls himself John Turner because it sounds more American.

The aforesaid Turner strides up and down the set frowning fiercely. He wears a small black cylinder on a length of cord round his neck. He can look through this and see what the camera sees.

Last night he spent much of the time sizing up the job, and we are all a little subdued. You would imagine it was Cecil B. De Mille planning how to get 20,000 extras up the side of a pyramid.

'Ready when you are, John,' says the chief operator.

'Hold it a minute, I'll be right with you.'

And he goes on with his pacing. The set measures all of three yards by four and everything is going to be filmed in that space. Even this area seems too much for him.

Suddenly Cecil B. Turner demands: 'I want the two kilowatt right away.'

'Ok, it's just above your bonce.'

'I want a back-light on Galia's hair when she comes in.'

'Fine, cock, but it'll take an hour to fix it.'

Turner is clearly annoyed at such familiarity on the set. He stretches to his full height and bellows: 'For Chrissakes, who's supposed to be directing this picture? How the hell we can get anything done in this...'

The electrician snarls through his dangling cigarette: 'Eh, do I shift the two kilo or don't I?'

'Oh leave it where it is,' growls Turner. 'We'll forget the back-light.' He takes up his stance and peeks through his black cylinder, then moves towards the door where I am to make my entrance. 'It'll be alright,' he declares.

The electrician stubs out his cigarette with a foot: 'Buggering about over a bloody two kilo...'

John T. bellows forth anew: 'Right everyone, we'll run through just once. Positions, silence!'

Turner takes me by the arm and explains the first scene. I am to appear in the doorway and exclaim: 'Oh hullo. Sorry to disturb you.'

Turner: 'Quiet! Galia, try it.'

'Oh hullo. Sorry to disturb you.'

'No lovey. Your second sentence comes too quick. Take a pause, look surprised, they're in bed naked, and then you say "Sorry to disturb you." OK? Try it again. Galia!' He flings a finger at me.

'Oh hullo.' Pause. 'Sorry to disturb you.'

'Great! She's got what it takes, our Galia. Positions, you stay at 18, you pan slow right, quiet please, roll 'em.'

'Roll 'em.'

'Title!'

The assistant-cameraman says: '*Charlotte et Ses Pelottes* scene one. Oh shit, wrong film. Sorry Mr Turner.'

Turner: 'For crying out loud, you don't have to say the whole damn title, just *Charlotte*. Do it again, quiet, roll 'em.'

'Roll 'em.'

'Title!'

'*Charlotte* scene one.'

I say my piece: 'Oh hullo.' Pause. 'Sorry to disturb you.'

'CUT!' yells Turner. 'Perfect, well done Galia, you should go far. We'll just do a back-up.'

The whole procedure gets into motion again and I say: 'Oh hullo.' Pause. 'Sorry to disturb you.'

July 5

Events are moving ahead fast at the College for Women. Gérard, Cyril and Hughes are treated by us all like precious objects, mascots, lucky medals.

We touch them, we fondle them, we breath them, we venerate them. They are the Ideal Man in Triplicate, the Erotrinity, the Three-Pronged Stronger Sex!

Gérard plays his part to perfection, Hughes acts like a total blockhead and Cyril lowers his eyes in modesty.

After several undressing cycles, our live males appeared at last in their naked glory. The audience got its money's worth. Their equipment was superb, each with a massive long phallus and a scrawny bag underneath with two well-defined bulges. Our men exuded health and strength. We all stared greedily at their manly credentials.

I was finding it hard to keep my legs closed. We had practised with the droopy rubber penis and with the hard rubber penis. And now we were moving onto the real thing! With real men!! We were positively drooling. The men got dressed again.

Madame De Chaussoy quietened us down: 'Now let us go back to the other day when our companion comes home tired from work and lies down on the bed. You want to rouse him. How do you go about it? We shall now see if you have grasped it so far. Claudine take Hughes, Micheline you can have Cyril, Myriam take Gérard.'

A choke escapes from my immediate neighbour. Her dream chimpanzee has gone to a rival, and the blood drains from her face. She seems likely to break into hysterics.

Hairy Hughes lies down on his demonstration camp bed on the right, Gérard in the middle and Cyril on the left of the platform.

The three women start the undressing procedure again. Myriam giggles a bit, Micheline is all fingers and thumbs with the buttons and zips, Claudine plods along methodically like a little girl playing with her doll. We were all waiting for her, as she carefully folded each article of clothing.

Our men lay naked on their beds, and the entire hall held its breath. I dared to glance around me. My fellow students were licking their lips, panting, shifting on their perspiring rumps, their whole bodies expectant. I had never seen so many randy women at one time.

Cho-Cho: 'Ladies, remember what you have learned so far. Yes, Myriam?'

'Madame, can we go right through with it, I mean can we – er – allow our partner – er – to ejaculate?' Even she was nervous.

'There would be no basic objection to that.'

My neighbour turned green. She was about to scream and I whispered urgently: 'Take it easy, you can collect him afterwards. It's a lesson, not real lovemaking.'

Cho-Cho: 'You can begin, ladies.'

Six hands surged forward and began touching lightly, stroking, feathering from feet to head. You could have heard a pin drop. Two of the women had certainly learned their rudiments, for Hughes and Cyril were erect in seconds. Flushed with victory, Claudine and Micheline took the penises in their mouths, removed them again and began licking. By now the men were expectant.

Myriam was in trouble, however. She tried again and again, using every. trick in the book. So much for *her* experience.

'Come on Gérard, be a sport, what's happened to you?' she scolded.

'Nothing.'

'You can say that again!'

She licks more eagerly, lifting his scrotum so that the skin is stretched and shining.

'For God's sake concentrate,' she orders. Gérard sits up and whispers in her ear. 'Well don't make such a fuss about it,' she snaps. She pinches the root of his penis, but to no avail. 'What do you want me to do?' He whispers again and she says: 'Well why didn't you say so in the first place!' Myriam resume her tongue work and sneaks a finger into his bottom.

At last his member springs to life, she envelops it with her generous lips and her head jolts several times in a swallowing motion. She stands back choking, and scurries off the platform looking neither to left nor to right.

July 7

We did some more filming in the sweltering heat. The air-conditioning has broken down, but fortunately we are wearing almost nothing. These scenes start with the classic preliminaries.

My opening greeting is answered by Gérard: 'Not at all, we are delighted to see you, come right in.' Mickey Mouse would have said it better.

Nadia adds: 'Why of course, come and sit down.' Nadia is more of a professional but the action just doesn't come across. It's not my problem, and I sit on the edge of the bed. They both start pawing me and undressing me.

The dialogue is unbelievably crummy:

'Mmmm, your pussy is lovely!'

'Yes, yes, yes, yes.'

'Oo, I'm all sticky.'

'Me too, ooh, ooh.'

'Put it in, *chérie*, put it in.'

'I'm going to, I'm sliding it in!'

This is easier said than done. We girls have Myriam's trouble on our hands, and we hear John Turner bawling out: 'Hurry up Gérard, get a hard on, any way you like, but get a hard on.'

Nadia knows her business and gets to work on him, and I lie spreadeagled on the bed. Gérard exclaims: 'I've got it in' and I cry out 'I can feel it sliding in!' Indeed I can and I get ready for the climax. It's taking longer than I thought and the sweat is pouring off us: 'I'm coming, I'm coming!' He's a good bluffer anyway, he couldn't ejaculate to save his life right now. He works too hard, I am thinking. 'I'm coming, oh it's spurting!' I hope he's right.

'CUT!!' We all fall back exhausted. Turner says blandly: 'Not too bad, Gérard. Nadia, give it more punch when you say "Put it in". Quiet roll 'em.'

'Roll 'em.'

'Title.'

'*Charlotte* 27.'

'Put it IN, *chéri*.'

'I'll put it in, I'll put it in!'

'CUT!' John leaps out of the shadows: 'How the hell can

113

you put it in when you can't get it up. You're shrivelled! Fix it, Nadia.'

Gérard looks like a character from *Les Misérables* but within a minute we are into *Charlotte* 28 and the scene ends with us all thrashing around gargling: 'Ah, mmm, ah ... yes, yes ... there, there ... mmm, *chérie chéri* ... I'm coming ... Ah Charlotte ...'

'CUT!!That's great kids. We'll take 30. I want you all back here in half an hour sharp.'

At the bistro four doors away we order a beer and *croque-monsieur* (what else!).

The male star is disconsolate: 'It's no good, I'll never make it to the end of the picture. I'm flaked out.'

Perfidiously I say: 'But you don't even ejaculate, so you ought to be springy. You tire yourself out too early on.'

'It's the College for Women, they are all sex mad there, they've cleaned me out. And all for a pittance. I can't go on like this.'

Nadia says: 'Ask the Directress for a few days off.'

'She'd never have that, the dragon! You ought to see her, she'd pull my balls off.'

'Go on sick leave, think of anything, say you've got the pox.'

A bright light flickered in the eyes of our weary stallion: 'Hey that's an idea, the pox! Great! Galia, promise you won't let on. You won't split on me?'

I tell him he can count on me, and Nadia says he's got to complete this film.

When we get back there is a power cut.

Turner is tearing his hair out: 'I don't believe it, I don't believe it, who is this damn fool of an electrician they've landed me with?'

The damn fool takes it in his stride, fiddling with his cables, a cigarette stuck to his lower lip.

The boss chides him: 'Come on buddy, get your finger out, we got a take on our hands. Oh for crying out loud!'

The electrician: 'Listen buster. Just keep it low, eh? I can't stand noise. Second, just let me get on with it; there's a short and I'm finding it. Third, if you want me to walk off the set just keep on shouting and I'll go and take a wander 'cos I've had a bellyful.'

Mr Hollywood from Brioude, Haute Loire, buttons his lip. He concedes: 'Forget it, we're all boiling over. Let's leave Paul with his short-circuit and run over the material. There's a candle on that shelf over there. Now, we're coming to close-ups and close-ins, Gérard on his back, Galia on her back on top of him, he is stuck into her' – this is starting to worry me – 'Galia opens up and Nadia moves in with plenty of action.' Nadia gives me a wink, I'm even more worried.

'What do we say?' I murmur.

'There's nothing written down. Do your own thing. Ah! The lights! Come on kids, positions. And you Gérard, a nice fat beat – see.' He signals to Nadia to handle it.

We are right into the hard stuff now, the camera is two feet from my vaginal entrance, I am sandwiched between Gérard who is mumbling, 'What a lousy job, what a lousy job' and a sparkling Nadia whispering 'Do you like this Galia, it's turning me on.'

John Turner is prancing round conducting us like he is Herbert Von Karajan. 'Get a beat, get a beat,' he orders Gérard.

On account of the power cut, we do not finish until 1 a.m. and are too tired even for a last drink.

July 8

Rumbles of discontent are sweeping through the College. The men are in open revolt saying they are not animals. Even the kindly Cyril says: 'You are asking too much.'

The ladies are exhausting the lads with their ministrations, extracting the very life from them. But they won't stop, they want more. Fights break out as they jostle for their turn to mount the steeds.

Madame De Chaussoy would like to bring in replacements, but she is worried about her budget, that is obvious. Gérard goes sick, and says what he has got.

'We'll catch it,' several women cry out. The entire project is heading for disaster.

July 10

I am not ashamed to confess that I go over the top in some of the *Charlotte* scenes.

The heat of the projector lamps, Nadia's lubricious lapping, Gérard's thrusts (yes, he can make it!) cause me to cry out in ecstasy. Which is precisely the moment when Johnny boy decides to cut. When I play-act and screech like a demented goose he keeps the cameras rolling. He's kinky.

July 11

The men have gone on strike at the College, and as with every strike the public are angry.

Some very fierce arguments break out, and I am amazed to see these extremists transformed into blind Furies calling for blood.

Cho-Cho does her best to quieten them down with lectures on the general theory of sexuality and its history, but the students won't have it.

They are haggard with frustration, they want their men back.

July 13

Charlotte is finished and we have seen the rushes.

We watched them in a tiny dust-laden room stinking of stale tobacco smoke, and I was absolutely horrified at what I saw. The picture has been synchronized but not edited. Turner says there will be hardly any editing.

The result is appalling – alignments quite amateurish, flat lighting, inaudible speech, washed-out colours. And there simply isn't a story.

'Well, what do you think?' says John Turner when the lights go up. Even he looks a little shamefaced.

'Looks great to me,' says Gérard. 'Fast pace, plenty of rhythm, should go like a bomb.' Pity there wasn't a bomb under him, I'm thinking.

'Nadia?'

'I think it's really very good, yes, very erotic. The scenes with Galia are terribly exciting. She has a wonderful body.' Nadia is actually leering at me.

'And you Galia, how do you feel?'

'I think it's a disaster.' Nobody says a word, and then John waves for me to go on. 'Everything is hopeless: camera work, soundtrack, decor, the whole shape of the thing. We are not people but just ridiculous mechanical fucking machines. There's not an ounce of imagination in the picture, not a grain of humour, not a glimmer of life. It's like a butcher shop with the meat jumping around. It's not even shitty, it's merely devoid of any interest.'

A glum silence. I can see my 4,000 francs disappearing over the hill; pity I did not ask for an advance. Ah well, too bad, but I refuse to cringe.

'So that's your opinion of my picture?'

'Yes,' I pout, and then slip my top lip over the other.

The boss scratches his head pensively, looks at us one after the other, and slowly fetches a bottle of whisky over. He hands out glasses and we drink in silence.

'Galia is right,' he says quietly. 'This picture is a wash-out. And I've made 15 other wash-outs. The only reason I go on is that I have no choice. I have a wife, four kids and a house to support. I have always wanted to direct real films, with real decors, outside shots, action, something with life to it. I would have done Western pictures, crime stories, adventure, Robin Hood, exciting chases, suspense, with hundreds of extras, big names. I never had the opportunity and I haven't the talent. So I do porn. You've noticed sometimes I have faith in that silly little set and I play at film-making too. But

I'm no fool, I know we produce crap. I agree with you Galia.'

I get up and walk over to him, giving him a big sloppy kiss on his forehead: 'Sorry John-John, I didn't want to hurt you . . .'

'You can call me Léon, that's my name.'

July 15

The College is in an uproar. A disgraceful incident occurred today when a minority group of the women tried to force the three men to halt their strike action. Not for the first time. And again it was to no avail, for the lads are demanding fixed hours and improved conditions, not more than one woman per hour, and beer breaks.

'You sort it out with the management,' the women scolded. 'You have been taken on to do this specialized work, it's a contract, you can't hold us to ransom!' Hughes gives them a two-finger sign.

'We'll go back when we have written undertakings,' Gérard said. Cyril fluttered his eyelashes in agreement, and even his doe-eyes have a militant look about them.

'We'll see about that,' Valentine snapped. 'Get back to work and stop messing about.'

A group of three seized Gérard and started tearing off his clothes, he fights them off with a few back-handers and more women move in. Hughes and Cyril stand by Gérard but the men are losing ground fast.

Then they started dealing out punches. Fists are flying from both sides, and the noise is infernal. Cho-Cho barges in and grabs the women one after another by their necks.

'Stop this, the lot of you!' she roars.

The punch-up subsides and Cyril is spitting out blood from a cut lip. Gérard's clothes are in shreds and Hughes cannot open one eye. Some of the women are pretty dishevelled too, and they stand back glowering at the three men and rubbing their wounds.

Myriam and I are horrified. We are disgusted with the

turn of events. The yapping dies down and Madame De Chaussoy walks onto the platform, she surveys the extremists, some of whom are locked in battle with the moderates. But the pushing and shoving comes to an end, and we prepare for the masterful Cho-Cho to put us in our place. But she does not shout this time.

She says in an even voice: 'As the result of this unruly incident, the College will be closed until further notice.'

The entire hall freezes. The news sinks in and suddenly some women begin patting the men, wiping their cuts with their hankies, kissing them better, crying and sobbing and trying to make amends.

'I'll run out for some iodine,' a middle-aged lady says. 'Let me heat some water, that needs a poultice,' moans another.

The three males allow themselves to be pampered, the women are back in their element, looking after their menfolk, unstinting in their duty. It's all lovey-dovey again.

Myriam and I exchange astonished glances. The women have all turned into nurses, and there is no sign of the hideous shrews of minutes ago.

Which goes to prove what I have always contended, that, for women, sex is a thing apart.

July 17

It is true that I have just had my 21st birthday, but I am as agitated as ever, dissatisfied physically, constantly on heat. It's terrible.

I have this powerful urge that I cannot control, I need the Great Unknown, I have an irresistible longing for debauchery. A bell seems to tinkle inside me and I am a Pavlovian dog.

There are millions of women, men too probably, who immediately snuff out any desire in themselves, especially if they think it is wrong. They keep control, sublimate it, argue it out in moral terms, avoid risk like the plague.

I am exactly the opposite. Temptation, the fire in my

entrails, the torrent of bestial desire – all this I love. Oh, how I adore the craving when it comes! It's a drug and I have to have sex.

It happened last night during dinner with Matthieu, Myriam and Gérard.

'I say we go on to *Le Bassano*,' I announced. Already I am breathing heavily and a sensual huskiness accompanies my statement.

'*Le Bassano*, where's that?' Matthieu asks.

'You don't know?' says Myriam. 'Never heard it mentioned? But my dear old fellow you've spent too much time in your Chinese cooking. You should live with your epoch, take a refresher course.'

'What about *Le Bassano*?'

'It's a sex club,' I tell him. The very thought of it is turning me on.

'A what club?'

'S-e-x.'

'What's that mean?'

Myriam is annoyed: 'A place where people fornicate!'

Matthieu: 'You mean they need a club for that?'

'Oh come on, you'll see. Coming Gérard?'

'I'm off my form at the moment, and in any case it's too expensive, 400 francs a glass of whisky. Sorry there's a limit.'

'Be my guest,' Myriam coos, obviously as sex-starved as I am. It must be the wine.

'Sorry, another time.'

So we eventually leave, just the three of us: Matthieu, Myriam and I.

At *Le Bassano* the eye of the manager is even more bloodshot than ever. So is his nose, in fact I think he must have cirrhosis of the nose. People have a horror of suicide, and the bottle is less forbidding than the gun. But the result is just as awful.

'Ah Galia, our little princess,' he growls. He has 70° proof coming out of his ears, but he remembers names. He leads us to the bar, and I experience a surge of nostalgia at this return to my starting point for Big Sex.

I hoist myself somehow onto a stool. These ones are designed for tall men with thin bottoms, another phallocrat trick as we spread when sitting on the stools and our thighs are forced apart. Myriam and I don't look too bad, almost rivalling Marlene Dietrich.

'Haven't seen you for ages, Galia,' says the blue nose. 'How's your friend from Italy, so charming: Eduardo or Octavio isn't it?'

'Osvaldo, he's just fine. He's with a Canadian girl about half my age, and he loves her.'

'And you?'

'Oh me . . .' I wave a hand in a gesture that says I'm alone, not in love, I adore men but not just one, and Emmanuel was my last chance.

'How about a starter?'

'Something nice and strong, but not whisky. Business looks thriving by the look of it.'

'Plenty of action, that's true. But plenty of cops too. They are calling now every month, they must be underpaying them. It's a real scourge of our times, this inflation. But we survive.'

I am delighted to see that the place is nice and full, and it seems like the orange room is overflowing. As we sit there, we see several rear quarters flit past the doorway: big ones, little ones, droopy ones (ugh), round ones (mmmm!) belonging to who knows? Civil servants, secretaries, captains of industries, priests, call girls, generals' wives . . . It may be seeing them, or perhaps the Armagnac, but my tummy is getting mellower minute by minute.

Then I can wait no longer: 'Coming in Myriam? Coming in Matthieu?'

My companions enter slowly, but I commandeer the bed in the middle. The male fraternity catch on quickly as I lie prone, kicking my legs invitingly. Some recognize me, and before long I am surrendering myself to their every whim. Some take me on my back, others when I am on my tummy,

121

others force me onto all fours and we play doggies. One middle-aged man rips his veined and full-ridge penis into my anus and I cry out, but at the same time he pinches a nipple and rubs me hard just above my clitoris and the pain becomes exquisite. I feel I am one huge sore, and that my anus is going to burst.

At moments I can see men waiting, masturbating like monkeys as they prepare for their turn. Little is said, but a young man protests: 'Excuse me, I was before you.' The other retorts: 'Pardon me, I've been here nearly 10 minutes!' He has trouble keeping his thing hard, and I quip: 'Too much of it makes you deaf.' He should know, he looks about 70, and when he mounts me he puffs and blows in my ear, concentrating for all he is worth. At last he utters a long groan and collapses on me like an eiderdown. I am shaking uncontrollably by now and rolling in a sticky pungent mess. I choose that moment to whisper: 'I didn't dare tell you, but I have syphilis.'

I am past caring, my sex is twice its normal size, I have had orgasm after orgasm and the craving has gone. In a dream I gather up my dress, my bra and G-string, someone hands me my shoes amid thanks. I stagger over to Myriam and Matthieu who are near the doorway and collapse into Myriam's arms.

'It was wonderful to watch,' she tells me bright-eyed. 'Sodom and Gomorrah was never like this. I came just looking.'

'It's purely physical.'

'Confucius here was explaining that the bacchanalia of ancient times achieved quite another dimension. He finds it rather sad, this club.' Her words underscored one certain fact: Matthieu was not really with us in spirit, and as she spoke he was looking at the fish in a tank next to the door.

I sat by him: 'We have to make do with the bacchanalia we've got. It's hardly our fault if we live in a society of decadents, whose idea of adventure is to drive up and down highways. You can criticize the people here as much as you

122

like, but you will never convince me that these places are not necessary. Whether it's a knocking shop or a private sex party, we have to have it. Where else are we to let off steam and get back to normal? Our civilization will not accept sin, the diabolical, the incongruous, the abnormal, the nonstandard. That kind of moral environment creates a huge build-up of tension and so you have to have places like this.'

Matthieu slowly raised his head: 'I don't need to let off steam. When I want to copulate, I copulate. If no-one's available I wait.'

A surge of anger went through me and I snapped: 'You're lucky, you're not abnormal like me. I need sex and sin and being naughty. I was born with a love of forbidden fruit, and that's how I get my thrills. I'm not saying it's right or wrong, but I have to have it. You can laugh, but I am really rather proud of the way I defend my pleasures.'

July 20

I am obsessed with sex, I think about it and want it all the time. I must have a new experience that is more daring than the last.

Yesterday I went on the rampage like an alley cat. In a small public garden at Denfert-Rochereau I egged on two total strangers in leather jackets, leading them behind a fence. I let them take down my knickers, I stood with my hands forward leaning against a statue, and let them have it off with me.

Later in the apartment block where a boy friend of mine lives, I got him to do it in the lift. Every time someone called the lift, I pushed the red emergency button to stop the lift. The danger of being discovered or the lift going wrong made it so much more exhilarating. Lifts are wonderfully secret and erotic places and they sway about too.

Last night another boy did it to me standing up inside an entrance porch in broad daylight. At any moment someone could have found us.

Myriam is as insatiable as I am, which is how we found ourselves today in a highly roused condition inside a sex shop in Rue de la Gaité in Montparnasse. We wore thin semi-see-through dresses and nothing underneath. People could see everything. I could feel every fibre of the material as it fluttered and wedged itself between my legs.

We went in slowly and found three or four men leafing through the literature. I glanced at some of the titles: *Schoolgirls On Heat*, *Toss Me Please*, *Vice Girls*. The men looked up as we sauntered in, and their tongues were almost hanging out. We were giving them something in the flesh to fantasize with. It would not have been half as fascinating for them had we been in the nude. Women know instinctively that desire can be infinitely more inflaming than the *fait accompli*!

Myriam and I approached one of the staff. I said in my cuddliest voice: 'We so wondered if you happened to have any – er – vibrators.'

'Vi... Yes of course, certainly *Mademoiselle*.' He can't have many bourgeoise customers.

The man fumbled behind the counter in a carton: 'These are ba-ba-ba-battery models.'

'Oh how nice, and how do they work?'

Fingers trembling, he showed us how to put the batteries in: 'You press the ON button and it works, it vibrates, you see.'

'Yes, but where is the best place to put it?'

'Pu-pu-pu-put it?'

Myriam helps out: 'Why don't you show us?' And she demurely drew up her dress with agonizing slowness, stood with her legs slightly apart and said: 'I hope it really does give relief.' She reached down and presented her genitals more prominently. The salesman had the machine in his hand and looked around at the other customers. Myriam said: 'Well come on, if we're going to buy one...' One of the bystanders had his hand in his pocket, and I saw the bump in his trousers moving.

A broad grin split the salesman's face: 'You're having a little joke with me, I can see, ha ha ha!'

'I am not joking, this is a serious matter, I need relief and be quick about it. Oh please!'

With calculated lasciviousness, but still pretending to be naive, she rolled her haunches ever so slightly, then said: 'Perhaps the other way round.' Myriam turned and bent forward a little, lifting her hem. She showed a beautifully rounded bottom, and I wondered how any man could resist her.

One of the customers saw his chance and grabbed the vibrator, trying to introduce it between Myriam's legs.

'Oh,' she sighed. 'But do be careful, lower down. Push the button, yes that's just right. Oh it's lovely, Galia we must buy it. Oh, it feels delicious.'

The salesman's mate is now guarding the door, and Myriam has ceased all pretence. She holds onto the counter and grits her teeth, throwing her head to right and left. We are all touching ourselves when she has her climax.

A few minutes later we left with our packet. We did not actually say it, but we both knew why we had done that in the shop. It's nice being a woman when you can tease. And it is so easy, because there are so many frustrated men, and most women won't dare make advances to men even though they want sex just as badly.

July 25

The vibrator has roused us both to fever pitch, Myriam and me.

Today we were in the Metro, and between Chatelet and Les Halles stations Myriam whispers to me: 'Do you think we are normal?'

'What's normal?'

'I don't know, like other people.'

'Then we're not normal. Look at the women in this carriage, they go out to work, have a husband, a fiancé or a

125

friend. They end up faithful spouses, good housewives, they have kids, build a home.'

Myriam giggles: 'We just have a hot stove, and you know where.'

'Do you envy them? Their fire is out, they spend all day doing their duty, conjugal or otherwise, getting meals, cleaning...'

'There's something to be said for a loving man who gives you reassurance. Is ours the next station?'

'No, two more. You know Myriam, I am keeping a diary, a sort of notebook.'

'Yes?'

'I write down everything that happens. I started it when I began to be sexually emancipated, when I was with Osvaldo. I thought it would help me work things out.'

'And are you keeping it going? Am I in it?'

'Of course, Myriam.'

'What do you write?'

'Everything that happens to us. The College, *Le Bassano*, the vibrator, everything.'

'Ooh! Has anyone seen it?'

'Oh no, you're the only one to know.'

'Darling Galia, I want to kiss you. Kiss me.'

We clung to each other in the swaying carriage, and kissed tenderly, sensually, desperately.

As we come out of it, a smart guy says: 'Another pair of cunt-suckers.'

His pal returns derisively: 'Lesbians, they're everywhere, what with Women's Lib and all...'

We flash loving messages to each other with our eyes, as we step off the train, holding hands.

III
DEBAUCHERY

September 2

After a long gap, I have decided to resume this diary and relate the *Roi-Henri* episode.

This is a villa perched on a hill in the snooty Western suburbs of Paris, right next to the Parc de Saint-Cloud.

The host and his wife receive guests in a rather dignified style. The old timbering gives the villa the appearance of a hunting lodge.

And hunting is indeed what the rendezvous is about. The huntsmen are numerous and not all hale and hearty. The 'game' is not always easy to find, and the males are famished.

The host lacks the friendly haze of the boss at *Le Bassano*, and is more like Alain Delon, the film star, in appearance. This sort of man has always attracted me and made me afraid at the same time.

I felt terribly vulnerable as soon as I was in the room. All eyes were on me, there was no standing on ceremony, not even a drink for the 'prey'. The female, that's little me on this occasion, enters the ring and the huntsmen size her up. There is a rich masculine odour of wild beasts, shirt sweat, leather, sperm.

The men standing in the shadows look at me crudely. I arrived with a man friend but he fades out at once, free to run riot if he wants with the hunters' own females. 'She's nubile... marvellous eyes... lively... what's she like from the back?' The comments are to the point, everyone knows why they are here.

Then suddenly, two steely-eyed men with slit mouths take my dress off, quickly but politely because these are distinguished people. And immediately several pairs of hands are pawing me, lightly pinching my bottom, thighs and breasts. I look this way and that, and they know my fear is half-genuine. I see several men unzipping their trouser fronts, but they keep their trousers on, so that they do not lose their dignity, maintaining their superiority over the female. They take out their penises, and most of them are already gorged and hard. Then the first one comes at me, two colleagues hold me down by my arms and the man sires me brutally. Then there is another and another. There is nothing romantic about it, and I feel humiliated. Even when a woman submits to being ravaged, she likes to be treated as a human being. This was too close to real rape, it was sadistic.

I left with my escort soon afterwards.

My legs were like cotton wool, I felt a wreck, I was still soggy, but I said: 'Let's walk a bit, I need air after that.'

There was a keen breeze on this early autumn evening and the woods were redolent of newly fallen leaves and of the good earth. I leant on my man, a friend but no more than a friend. I wanted to cry but I held it back.

I still feel uncomfortable about the *Roi-Henri* incident, and he is reserved.

September 3
Myriam is worried about me, and told me about a sexologist

a girl friend of hers heard about. To tell the truth I am
running a little scared myself.

'He's called Dr K and he practises in Rue de Vaugirard.
Why not give him a call, go and tell him about your
problems? He may be able to help.'

I phoned for an appointment with Dr K and he fixed up to
see me the same day, which was yesterday.

He is about 50, has thick black eyebrows, seems nervous
and speaks in short rushes.

As soon as we are alone, he orders: 'Take your clothes off,
I will examine you.'

Shocked, I blurt out: 'But I have not come to see you for
any physical trouble. That side of it is perfectly in order.'

'Organic, psychological, everything is linked. Undress
please.' He is extremely grumpy and I am not sure I like him.

Truculently I observe: 'If you think you can find my life-
style problems in my vagina, you are an optimist.'

'Get undressed!'

I decide to dig my heels in, after all this is a genuine
consultation: 'I'm sorry, I don't see the necessity.'

'As you wish,' he growls. 'Well, what's the difficulty?'

This is not an easy question to handle on the wrong side of
the desk from an irritable man who keeps tapping the desk
and shifting in his chair.

'I would like to know what is normal and what is not in the
matter of sex.'

'Can you be more precise?'

'Well, for example, is it normal for a woman to want
sexual relations with a lot of men?'

'How many?'

'Well, I don't really know, I haven't kept count.
Sometimes I go for three or four days or even a week, and
then make love in a day or a night with, say, 10 men.'

'I beg your pardon?'

'With 10 or 12 or perhaps 6. I mean, almost continuously.'

The consultation lasted about five minutes. Then Dr K
wrote out a prescription in a rapid hand and thrust it at me:

'That will be 200 francs.'

I read what he had written down: *Two tablets Tranxène 5 three times daily. During crises one Valium 10 tablet. Relations twice weekly maximum.* My face dropped.

'Come and see me again in two weeks' time.'

'Certainly not! Here are your 200 francs, but I'd like to ask you a question first.'

'Yes?'

'In your view... Hey, are you listening?'

'I am.'

'In your view, is it dishonesty or stupidity that drives you on?' He is nonplussed and I add: 'I would guess it is stupidity. But you've got your 200 francs just the same, haven't you?'

September 5

Osvaldo phones, inviting me out for a party flung by 'a famous and remarkable and enthralling friend.'

I retort: 'Why don't you take your Canadian girl?'

'I couldn't do that, it's not the sort of evening for her. You know what I mean, she hasn't the style, the experience...'

Huffily I rant: 'You feel better with your old flame for a saucy evening, is that it? You don't want to contaminate your nice tender little girl with the barbarians. But you still want to have a dirty evening once in a while, and old Galia will suit just nicely!'

'Oh Galia, don't be silly, you...'

'I'll come on one condition: it must be good entertainment. If it's another miserable routine gallop, count me out.'

Osvaldo switches on the honeyed Caruso voice I know so well: 'Galia, I promise you'll love it, real entertainment, I'm not joking. Say you'll come, I need you.'

'Alright then.'

'Oh wonderful! Galia, I'll love you for ever. You are the most stupendous, the...'

'Don't climb up the curtains, as they say in Quebec. What do I wear? I'd prefer jeans to a ball gown.'

'You'll be wearing a peplum.'

'A what?'

'A Roman peplum. It's a flimsy white thing with a hole for your head and one for each arm. Nothing else of course.'

'And where am I suppose to acquire a peplum, if you please?'

'Everything will be supplied on the spot.'

It was well organized, and for an excellent reason. When Osvaldo introduced me to the host, I blinked and blinked again.

I recognized the creased laughing eyes of this 50-year-old personality known to the whole of France. In less than a split second my mind wrote out the story of his life: baby's bottle, potty, fingers in the jam, snatching small brother's toys, kicking nurse, giggling at nurse from the bath, touching his little penis for the first time, kissing his cousin under the apple trees, spluttering with a cigarette, sucked off in the Bois de Boulogne as a teenager, first real girl friend, she dumps him, second girl friend, and so on. Yes, I knew him! It's R. D., the T.V. and radio joker who runs the 'Musk and Truth' show on the radio.

'Delighted and honoured to have you with us,' he beams, taking my erotic temperature with a flick of his eyelashes.

'I listen regularly to your programmes,' say I. (My God, Galia, what a liar you are. You heard it once in a taxi stuck in a traffic snarl. The 'Musk' programme, of indescribable banality, consists of openings by fatty R.D. on the lines of 'And for you, what is happiness?', 'And for you, what is Man?', 'And for you, what is love?', 'And for you, what is wealth?'. He must have done about 5,000 programmes, all as pathetic, treacly and alienating as the one before. R. D. is the unctuous confessor of the French nation.)

'Come right over,' he croons. 'You must meet everyone.'

He takes me over to a third rate pop singer I recognize, one willing to flirt with anything risky as long as it sells his latest album: 'Galia, but she's bee-ootiful!'

A young neuro-psychiatrist, charming, twisted face and

probably nymphomaniac.

Next a ginger-haired fellow with a curl that keeps falling forward. I would like to lend him a hair-slide and wonder whether he runs on wind or sail power or both.

A blessed relief, I shake hands with a girl student aged 18 or 19, pretty and likeable at sight, obviously the carefree kind.

A businessman, ugly like most of them. The job makes, or deforms, the man, and in this case the result is grisly.

Another businessman, not quite so grisly no doubt because business is bad, with his lawful wedded spouse who keeps tittering and nattering about the weather in the park.

After that I am presented to a curious moon-like creature with a grey complexion seeping through her make-up. She has saucer eyes of a deep black. I am not surprised to hear her named as Stella.

Finally, there is the pearl of the evening: a tall striking beauty with natural grace. Large blue eyes, chestnut hair and a truly superb pair of legs. I gather she is our host's partner, for this evening at least.

R. D. then takes Osvaldo and me to our room, where the first thing we see are two immaculately white peplums. (Pepli? Pepla? I should have looked it up perhaps.)

'Well, I'll leave you to get changed,' says R. D. in his impeccable bronze voice. A round-the-clock professional is our R. D.

Dinner by candlelight with all of us in peplums, served by two adorable English girls disguised as Napoleon's grenadiers, which seems tough on them. They are wearing black trousers and golden jackets with frogs and loops, and have mustaches crayoned under their noses so that they look like twins.

'May I help you to some more consommé?' they ask in their delightful cross-channel accent. We can hear the question go right round the table in a sort of cotton-wool tone.

'I could eat grenadiers like that any day,' says the uglier of the businessmen, trying to get the party going.

'So would I,' shouts the pop singer, but then he would do anything as long as it sold another cassette.

'And you, Galia, how about two little grenadiers for you?'

The joke is already thin and I simply reply: 'I have a horror of anything military, but I think these two soldiers could change the views of any pacifist.'

And so it goes on for a while, with everybody well-behaved and respectable. I wonder when the perfect subjunctives will give way to the perfect whoop-up. The film of good manners seems fairly thin.

The answer comes with the grilled lobsters. The salient feature of the peplum is that it has gaps and the wearer is semi-bare on each side; and the thing about lobsters is that you have to wave your arms about as you tug, crack and gouge out the beasts with a variety of implements including fingers. Inevitably the garments ease open to reveal the ladies' breasts, and from that point onwards there is no holding back the men. Or the women. Wine flows freely as male hands insert lobster nippers into our yawning garments and fingers accidently press our nipples. Arms advance around our shoulders to help us with our lobsters and lose their way in our folds. The women make a fuss of being embarrassed, but it fools no-one, and in less than no time the pearl of the evening is squatting on her haunches, peplum round her waist, calling for offers. Needing no further encouragement the neuro-nympho sidles over to the pop singer and gropes him generously. The less ugly of the two businessmen makes a dive for me and massages my breasts as his wife looks on breathing 'Ah, ah, ah.' Osvaldo is working on the girl student and the ginger fellow buries his head in Stella's orbs muttering about cybernetics.

Then everything stops as suddenly as it has started, and the dessert is brought in.

All in all it is an excellent dinner with stimulating wine and efficient service. Added to that, we have the promise of more licentious events to come.

Logs crack in the huge fireplace as the toy grenadiers clear the table. Everyone is bourgeois again. The men shift the table to one side, freeing a large area in the centre of the room.

Our host advances and, as solemn as an archbishop at his own enthronement, unhooks a cord that works a pulley system.

Unusually excited, Osvaldo murmurs to me: 'I promised you entertainment.'

A pregnant hush descends on us as the English girls stand to attention next to the rope. R. D. emerges with a whip and whirls it round and round over our heads. He leers at the girls and strokes their faces.

'You are she-dogs, aren't you?' he says.

'Yes, we are she-dogs,' they recite like schoolchildren.

'You are little bitches.'

'We are little bitches.'

'And you have lost the war.'

'Yes, we have lost the war.'

'And you deserve to be punished.'

'Yes, you must punish us.'

The whip circles again and we cringe.

'What shall we do, ladies and gentlemen, to punish these wicked she-dogs, so that they do not forget it?'

'Thrash them,' says the ugly businessman.

'Ah, ah, ah,' squeaks the silly wife.

'We shall give them the whip, beat and thrash these naughty she-dogs.' He reads strip cartoons in bed, I am sure. 'First we shall take their clothes off.'

Osvaldo assumes a sickly grin and advances to remove their clothing. He loves anything to do with teenage girls. He is showing his teeth like an overgrown boy scout who has won a badge.

The fancy tunics come off first, and we see the girls' white breasts, two little apples adorned with pink cherries. They tremble as Osvaldo bends down and takes their shoes off. He undoes their belts and slowly slides down their trousers with

136

their little white knickers inside. They step out of them and are completely naked. Osvaldo's eyes are shining.

The radio confessor lifts up their arms and ties their wrists together. They are prisoners back-to-back.

R. D. scowls and walks round the girls, threatening with the whip and licking his lips. He looks genuinely cruel.

He gives the whip a sharp crack, and the silly wife goes 'Ooh.' They ought to gag her, or she is going to spoil everything. We need complete quiet now.

Thwack – thwack – thwack the whip goes, and the two girls jump each time, their breasts shaking. I notice something else now, there is a bulge in the whipman's trousers. His eyes are glistening, he is sweating, twirling the whip faster and faster. He is in earnest and the cracks are getting louder. I look at Osvaldo's trouser front and see that he has a bump too.

I lean over to him: 'He won't really hurt them, will he? There'll be trouble.'

'I don't think so. He's done it before, and so have they, and the whip makes more noise than anything else. He got it in Japan.'

The dishy tall girl appears from nowhere, she stands in front of a spotlight, in her peplum, and we can see her curves outlined through the thin material.

'Have pity on them, please have pity on them,' she cries, loading on the emotion by the shovelful. She has a lovely voice.

R. D.: 'They are bitches, whores...' He really believes it. He is into strip cartoons up to his scrotum, and the make-believe lashes crash down. Lasciviously, I imagine I am a man and can turn this fantasy into reality, thrashing the girls so that they scream with pain. R. D. could do that and get away with it.

But the older girl rushes up to the English pair and hugs them. She flings off her robe and rubs her mound of Venus against one of the girl's pubic areas, then she does it to the other. What delicious bodies they have! But there is no time for me to ogle them, for the host has dropped his trousers and thrown the whip aside. He walks awkwardly towards the trio, his phallus hard and shiny. The veins are standing out.

At this turn of events the rest of us leap up. The men cast aside all attempt at courtesy and we of the feminine gender stand by and watch as the pop singer forces his penis into the vagina of one adolescent and the businessman pumps the other like a crazed bull. The poor mites, they are not fully developed and it must hurt them terribly. A whipping would have been better. I notice the idiot woman wrestling under a man, but we others are frantically trying to pair off now. We are all naked and can't restrain ourselves.

The show goes on until dawn, or rather the sideshows do. It would be easy to mock us. We could be dismissed as mentally unhinged, completely deranged, the scum of civilization. But we do no harm, and everyone is unhinged in some way, and all are sexually obsessed. If you are to make a distinction it should be between those who are obsessed WITH sex and those obsessed AGAINST it. The latter are the silent majority and they have won the battle so far.

Dawn comes at last, salmon pink and with its message of hope. The guests are eking out the last of the night's pleasure, but I go off on my own in the grounds of the house, away from the dirty glasses and cigarette butts and the garments strewn on the floor. I watch for a while as the sun comes up.

I am calm and I reflect that, in the realm of pleasure, anything is permitted provided it does nobody any permanent harm.

September 8

I am seriously worried about myself, anguished about the future. Last night I had another big session with a man I know, lasting hours and hours. Increasingly I need sex and I want it raw. I become frenetic, demanding multiple orgasms any way I can get them. Afterwards I flop around as if drunk. What does it signify? Am I mad and don't know it? This is no joke, being a slave to my racing libido.

The anguish takes on new urgency at the moment, because Myriam has actually started with an analyst.

I phoned her: 'Myriam darling, what's good for you must be good for me, because we are alike. I feel out in the cold. What's your chap's name?'

'He is a woman, she's called L. C.'

'Would you mind if I call her?'

'Of course not, *chérie*, how super to have the same analyst.'

Yesterday evening I put in a call to L. C. She was rather stuffy, saying she could not possibly treat us both, in view of our intimate relationship. It would upset the analytical process. To cut a long story short, she told me to look elsewhere.

I am getting desperate, so I do what she says. By chance (the experts in this field claim there is no such thing as chance) I come across someone in the ad columns of *Le Nouvel Observateur*, my old hunting ground. 'Analyzed by Lacan, fee depends on client's situation, ring 732.85.19.'

My appointment is for tomorrow at 4.30 p.m.

September 9

I have seen him. It was close by Vincennes Metro station, on the fourth floor, with the door stating simply 'R. Psychoanalyst'.

I rang the bell and the door opened to reveal a short man who waved me into his office. He's about five foot tall, not much more.

Her perches on his chair and flaps his hand at a seat on the other side of the desk. I slip into it and our conversation goes roughly as follows:

R: 'You wanted to see me.'

Me: 'Yes I saw your ad by chance in *Le Nouvel Observateur*.'

R: 'Perhaps it's not chance.' (Aha, I was right!)

Me: 'Well anyway, your ad reached me. I think that's the term.'

R: 'Say it how you like.'

Me: 'How would you say it?'

R: 'It's not my problem.'

Me: 'Alright then. I called you because I am wondering whether I ought not to start some analysis.'

He looks at me with every appearance of thinking. I am thinking he is pretending to.

Me: 'What do you think?'

R: 'About what?'

Me: 'About my idea of undergoing analysis.'

R: 'And what do you think?' (I am now wondering how long this little game is going on. Why do these people always answer with another question? Answer: why not?!)

Me: 'We could stop swapping questions maybe. It's too much like a fight.'

R: 'Why do you say "fight"?'

Me: 'Because it's like an indoor game where the winner is the one who gets in most questions, and the one who gives most answers is the loser. It's too easy playing that game and giving nothing away. I saw your ad, you are the one who took the first step, not me. So I'm the one to ask the questions, OK?'

R: 'That's not a question, it's a proposition.'

Me: 'It amounts to the same, don't be funny. You used this ad to fish for clients, patients or whatever. Why?' (If he says 'why not' I'm leaving.)

R: 'Call it fishing if you like. I am a psychoanalyst, my job is to listen to patients. I merely announced that I am here.'

Me: 'Why didn't you use a big display ad? A full page spread with the headline PSYCHOANALYST SEEKS PATIENTS? I want to know why you set up as an analyst. You could be a dentist, teacher, dancer, grocer, poker player or a stockbroker. An analyst, why? What does it achieve for you? What does it mean to you?'

R: 'What do you think?'

Me: 'That's enough! Enough questions and answers. I am making inquiries, I could become a client, I know nothing about analysis, I need to know what it is, how it works, what you do. You are in a specific job, and I want to know about it, what I am letting myself in for.'

R: 'If I explain what analysis is, I would lead you along a path you would not perhaps take on your own. Every analyst has his own way of helping the analysis along. It's not for me to say what psychoanalysis is, strange as that may seem.'

Me: 'So you are asking me to jump in blindly, into the unknown. Like Pascal said: "Kneel down and you will believe." You are saying: "Lie down and you'll see." I like to know where it's heading.' Especially the kind of couch where I shall be laying my head and resting my bottom. 'I need to know who you are, what your story is. All I know is that you have been analyzed by Lacan. So he's a big name. May I ask why you mentioned that in your ad? A quality reference perhaps? Meaning you've been properly analyzed yourself, lain on France's number one couch? What does that badge mean, "analyzed by Lacan"? What plus point does it give you that he's analyzed you? Extra know-how, super-power? Answer that!'

R glowers at me, I repeat the last question or rather the demand. He keeps on glowering.

Me continued: 'You stated it in writing "analyzed by Lacan" and that must mean something. I have a right to know what it means for you.' He remains tight-lipped. 'Good God, are you going to answer? Your pitch is too easy, you keep quiet and the patient fends for herself. Well it won't work with me. I have a right to know all about you as a practitioner.'

R: 'You have a right.'

Me: 'So you haven't lost your tongue. What's it mean "analyzed by Lacan"?' Renewed silence. 'What's it mean?' Silence. 'I demand a reply. Huh, so you won't reply.'

R: 'What would you like me to reply?'

Me: 'Ha, so we're back to the pussy-footing! Well you can

find someone else to love you, you and your question-answer game and your wise old neutrality, your small ad and your chocolate medal. You can stuff your couch, you cut no ice with me. Find some other victim in *Le Nouvel Observateur*. And good hunting!'

September 11

I am still mad at the dwarf analyst during the evening and I need to get him out of my system.

I have bugs in my panties and I show up at *Le Bassano* where the boss gives me a great big smile.

'On your own?'

'Yessir.'

'But...'

'There's no but. I ain't alone because I'm here. Dribble me out some of your firewater. I want to take off, fly round the world, be nice with everybody.'

He gives me a quick glance: 'I've got some good grass, if you're interested. Let me roll you a joint.'

'That's nice, but no thanks. Give me a brandy, and then I want to be laid. Any good stallions tonight?'

'It's a little early, people take a while to warm up. But there's a hot gringo from South America looks like he'd shoot at anything that moves.'

I down the brandy and stroll into the orange room. The first thing I see is the gringo playing at humpty-back with a large squashy woman in her mid-forties. The South American has a neat mustache across his mouth and plenty of not-so-neat hair everywhere else. Except on his head which is slicked down like Rudolph Valentino's. He is a big man, this is going to be quite an experience.

I can smell leather, the fragrance of raw skin, and I throw a husky 'Hullo hombre' at him. Slowly I gather up the skirt of my dress and lift it till I judge my lace curtains are just showing. (I felt like frilly things tonight, and it looks like I chose right.) He stops wallowing in the swamp and stares at

142

me open-mouthed. I close my eyes, swivel left and right, I have him in my power and I like it. I strip in professional style, and he gets up and rushes at me, fingering the lace on the only remaining article of clothing.

I goad him: 'I'm a better heifer maybe? Come on picador, show me how you do it. Let's see if you can ride me too.'

He really goes for this tarty act, and rides me in the customary position for a while with his jaws clamped firm, his black eyes shining.

This boy sure has muscles and he turns me over like a flapjack.

'You play bitch,' he croaks.

'I play bitch, *si signor*!'

He jams one hairy arm over my back, the other under my neck, so that my back arches to breaking point. His phallus edges between my vulva and goes on entering, he withdraws and then thrusts and thrusts repeatedly. I am entirely his and I can't savour enough of his meat. Never have I felt so raunchy. He is indefatigable and I want it to go on for ever. He doesn't come and I am glad. I glance about and now see a whole circle of spectators admiring our performance.

I wave a small pink-faced young man over to me: 'Please help me, bring me a triple brandy.' This he does and wafts it near me. 'Let me have it, let me have it, don't be afraid, I won't eat you.'

The picador releases me and I drink the brandy in one go, then he enters me again. The brandy sets me on fire and I imagine myself being sired by a donkey.

The young man is in front of me and my hands find his belt. He lets me undo it and I pull down his trousers, then his underpants. His little penis is pink too but limp, he puts it in my mouth and I make it harder, sucking and sucking and loving my power to make it harden. The two men are penetrating me, my mouth and my vagina. The brandy has rendered me frantic, and I can feel the gringo getting to monster size. This time I am at their mercy, being buffeted, and then they ejaculate together as I thrash about with my head wildly. I go into a pleasure-pain coma.

I can remember little of what followed, although it was only yesterday.

I do know that a naked man aged about 60 with a fine bronzed body put his head betweeen my thighs and that I jerked again and again. Others threw themselves on me and violated me. I remember seeing men masturbating and spurting over me. An auburn-haired woman with ginger fur laid back and showed me her sex, and I got up and put mine against hers imagining I had a penis, and we both came. I rolled my haunches forward and back pressing my clitoris against hers and rubbing and rubbing, and got off again.

I was completely drunk and lost count of the males who took me. One smelled putrid, probably hormone trouble. I provoked them and insulted them, and one protested: 'Not so loud mademoiselle, you can have us all but you must keep your manners.'

Mad with rage I got up and staggered against him, enveloping him in my arms. I got him on the floor, forced my tongue between his teeth, then grabbed his thing and chewed it. Then in a final gesture of defiance I stood over him with my legs apart and pissed all over his belly. Then I suppose I collapsed.

Never had I behaved as outrageously as I did last night. I lived the ultimate in sin and debauchery with every fibre of my body. My whole being was a red raw sex. I was going to hell and I did not care. I was in a state of despair.

September 14

Today I made another attempt to fix up an analyst.

This time I went to see a sober-looking man in one of the high-class avenues in the 17th *arrondissement*. The time was 3 p.m. and he had me shown into his office where I felt humble, almost contrite.

Below I give the conversation word for word, partly because I recall it clearly but also to cheer me up when I am old and grey.

'I asked to see you because M. L. gave me your name. I am wondering whether I ought to undergo a course of analysis.'

'The fee is 300 francs.'

'I beg your pardon.'

'Three hundred francs.'

'You mean each session costs 300 francs?'

'Quite so.'

'I'm afraid that is more than I can afford. I am a student and my father gives me a monthly allowance, but...'

'It's 300 francs.'

'So I understand. And the sessions last how long?'

'Why do you ask that question?' (Oh for pity's sake, we are into pat-a-ball again.)

'It's so that I can fit it in with my work, other activities...'

'Sessions are short ones, lasting no longer than 15 minutes.'

'If I come at 2 o'clock, can I be sure of getting away by 2.15?'

'Certainly, it's 300 francs.'

'I see. How many sessions a week?'

'Three.'

'Making 900 francs a week.'

'Quite so.'

'In other words 3,600 francs a month. That's more than my monthly budget. So with you I shall have to stop eating, buying clothes, and sleep in the open. How do you think I can manage that?' No answer. 'Could you arrange for a reduction, at least at first?'

'It's 300 francs.'

'Strange, but I was told that psychoanalysts adjust their fees to match their clients' incomes. That's why I'm asking for a reduction. The fee seems on the high side.'

The shrink glares at me, he does not move or speak, and we stay like this for a while.

I volunteer: 'At 300 francs per 15 minutes, you should be a rich man. Social security doctors don't even ask 60 francs for

15 minutes.' No reaction. 'Supposing you work eight hours a day, which would be the normal thing, you make 9,600 francs a day.' No reaction. 'With that kind of money, couldn't you take on some impoverished patients? Do you absolutely need nearly 10,000 francs a day?'

Calmly he replied: 'I am afraid our conversation is turning into an argument. I have said all I have to say. It's 300 francs.'

'Not for me. I prefer to remain neurotic than pay money to a crook. Good day to you.'

Setpember 15

I'm trying so hard. Another shrink, a woman.

About 30, brown hair, big doleful eyes that still missed nothing. On her desk a large photo of Freud with piles of his books including the *Gesammelte Werke* along with the English and French translations. A complete Sigmund library. And around stood his friends, disciples, pupils, traitors and renegades: Jung, Ferenczi, Rank, Groddeck, Adler, Abraham, Klein, Winnicott, Lacan and the others.

Hélène W. offers me a seat, and I sit on the edge of a couch. She comes over and sits by me.

'So you are thinking of starting analysis?'

'Yes.'

'Why do you feel the need?'

'I want to sort myself out, learn more about myself, try to put right some things that are not right and make me feel awful. I want some of the ache to go away and to feel better when I am fine. I want a better existence.'

'You're unhappy?'

'No. Yes. I don't know.'

'Perhaps you don't feel you are loved enough?' (Crash, the first wrong deduction!)

'I feel I am loved enough, loved too much in fact.'

'Are we ever loved enough?' says Hélène W., fingering back a long wisp of brown hair that is tickling her nose. A silence follows. All analysts without exception have the irreplaceable quality of knowing the value of quiet.

'Men, it's men,' I whisper. 'That's why I need analysis.'

A new interest appears in her expression: 'Do they do nasty things to you?' (Crash, number two error.)

'No, that is not the problem.'

'Tell me what the difficulty is, then.'

She seems disappointed. Her gaze is now tragic, and she reluctantly clears it away with fluttering lashes. It would certainly have suited her better if I had been beaten up by men, raped, sodomized by force, tortured or strangled. Unfortunately they have always been so nice to me.

'There are no difficulties,' I gulp.

'But you mentioned a problem.'

'I? Never!'

'Yes you did.'

'Oh no.'

'You said it was because of men that you needed analysis.'

'That's certainly true. But it's not strictly a problem.'

Actually I am not being quite honest with her, because I sense that it is not with her that I want to lay myself bare.

'You want sessions because of men...'

'Yes, because of them.'

'Why's that?'

'Because I despise them.' She falls to reflecting on this, linking facts, kicking them around, looking for symbols.

'Do you know why you despise them?'

'That's the trouble, I don't.' Her eyes are soft and tender, she smiles at me, moves a bit closer.

'Don't worry too much, we can sort all that out together...' (Crash, third error.)

Then I pour it out: 'I don't want an analyst who reassures me. Even before you start, you are crushing me with kindness. You want to help me and that in itself means you are not helping me. When I need comforting I go and see my friend Myriam, when I want to be petted I go with a male friend. I don't need tenderness, I need clear facts. You are

147

very kind, responsive and sympathetic, but I feel that if I started analysis with you, myself on the couch and you in the chair, we should soon be changing places.'

My lips expand into a sweet smile: 'I believe *you* are the one who needs lots of love, but I can't help you. Let me give you a big kiss, you are so nice.'

September 17

At 1 a.m. today, when all respectable people are in their own beds, Sylvain and I went in his car to Porte Dauphine on the edge of the Bois de Boulogne.

Sylvain, who has made love to me just once, has a small electric car. He drove slowly with about three thousand other cars with headlights on, round the main traffic island and then along the dark roads lined with hookers in net stockings, showing their breasts and beckoning to the drivers. This night as on so many others they sway their hips, blow kisses and heap scorn on the transvestites. Here the law of the sex jungle holds good, each animal defending its territory tooth and claw.

My escort slows the car alongside a sumptuous girl with long hair drawn back, superb lashes and long legs that peep tantalisingly through her brazen red slit dress. Her breasts are uncovered, firm, round and full. She has a perfect body, except that *she* happens to be a *he*, one of the many Brazilians who have been operated on. We stop and I wind down the window.

'Fifty for a suck, hundred for lovemaking,' he says in a melodious voice straight from the Sertão.

'Do you go with women too?'

He freezes a moment, leans forward to get a closer look at us. This is something new for him, a woman customer.

I extract myself from the midget car and take the 'girl' by the hand. She is taller than I am.

'Come on, Sylvain.'

'Er, sorry Galia, not my kind of trip.'

'Well wait there till I come back.'

Sylvain throws his head around left and right, worried. Shadowy figures move furtively from tree to tree, illuminated briefly as the headlamps show the woods.

'Alright, I'm tagging along,' says my companion.

'Afraid of the Big Bad Wolves?'

'Frankly, I'd feel better at my place or yours with the lights on, a drink, cushions, music.'

'Oh don't be silly, learn to live dangerously, it's something new. Hurry up, I can't wait.'

The Brazilian leads us under some branches and we reach a small deserted clearing. I fish out some banknotes and the Brazilian switches on a little torch to check them. He smiles broadly, it's more than enough.

'You want lovemaking?' You bet I do. He has an honest face, a gaze soft as velvet. I am longing to see the rest of him and I tell him.

'I want to see you strip, and then we'll try some improvisations.'

'Provisions?' The angel hardly understands French, and I squeeze his hand: 'Don't worry, we are nice people.'

He is so utterly erotic that I catch my breath. He unhooks the dress and lets it slide off languidly. He moves exactly like a real stripper, and even Sylvain releases a low whistle of admiration.

His panties are white and show up invitingly in the half-light. He keeps them on and moves his belly and hips sensually. My mouth is watering as I watch his dark body in its undulating dance.

He slows to a halt and theatrically whisks off his pants, throwing them a few feet away. The Brazilian stands still, with proud breasts heaving as he recovers from the dance. His penis is sticking out exactly horizontal in a semi-erection. The effect is sensational and Sylvain and I are unable to comment, such is our emotion.

Excited beyond measure, for this is really something bewitching, I feel the bitter-sweet desire in my loins. I take two steps forward.

He does not move when I touch him, caressing his whole body, avoiding his breasts. I kiss his right arm and play with his golden bracelet, drawing the hand past the elastic round my hips and placing it on my mound. The transvestite pulls his hand back in an instinctive gesture as his fingers make contact with my moist vaginal lips. I enclose his hand and try to show him how to fondle me. I realize then that he has never done this before, and my heart melts for him. It is like being teacher to a 10-year-old boy.

'How old are you?'

'Nineteen.'

'Where are you from?'

'Sao Paulo.'

'Have you ever made love with a woman?'

He shakes his head. Oh bliss! I want him, I want him, I want him.

I pull down my own panties and open my dress. I must go slowly and not frighten him. I kiss a shoulder the texture of moleskin and work my way to his breasts, taking a nipple hungrily into my mouth. I feel his penis and find that he remains half-cocked. This increases my desire. I want him to possess me, the urge is frantic and I gently rub my orifice against his sex in quick movements. But he remains in weak turgescence, his unruly member is exasperatingly uncooperative. I am desperately trying to get him up, thinking how marvellous it would be if I could get it off myself with this man-woman with the appeal of both male and female. I yearn to be penetrated by this bisexual as our breasts press together. I began fondling him more subtly, titillating him as I have done to men so often, but the more my desire increases the less he is stimulated.

'Don't you ever get hard? Concentrate! What's it for, what do you like?'

'Please men, not women,' he says.

'Sylvain it has to be you, come here.'

'But . . .'

150

'Stand here and let him do it.'

My escort opens his zip, the Brazilian kneels down and takes him into his mouth. Soon the transvestite's phallus stiffens and rises. I throw Sylvain aside and pull the man's shaft into me and it keeps firm. I ride it wildly, clinging to him hopelessly.

September 18

My head is a rushing torment of noise. Am I normal or beyond help? What is to become of me?

I know now that only treatment can save me, can give me the answers I must have.

Setpember 24

My debauched condition is worsening.

Close by Réaumur-Sebastopol Metro station two evenings ago, I walked the street clad in an outrageous mini-skirt and a see-through blouse. I have laid my make-up on thick, my lips are two red weals. Men fall in step behind me as I saunter along. The regular girls eye me with hostility, and I am scared of pimps. But at last a man comes up to me.

'What's your price?' He may be a pimp.

'Five hundred francs.'

His mouth turns down, I am obviously not worth it.

'Two hundred, in the car,' he mutters.

'What car?'

'Mine.'

I nod and follow him. In the passion waggon, he pokes me hurriedly as I lay sprawled diagonally on the back seat. I feel no emotion but grit my teeth, then leave him to look for another client.

Later in a nightclub in the 17th *arrondissement*, I shock everyone by starting a striptease act. I am groggy with drink, and they take me out. My male companion starts an argument over it, but we cannot get back inside.

151

I get as far as the *Katmichou*, where only women are allowed. I play the clown and appeal for partners. I remember attaching a celluloid penis to my loins, and going round the tables asking girls: 'Would you like it?' One or two nod, I walk forward with the thing and they help me introduce it.

In the early hours I stop a young couple in the street. I go straight up to the man and put my tongue into his mouth. They are flabbergasted, so I kiss the girl too. 'How about the three of us going to bed?' They march off briskly.

Then yesterday in the Luxembourg Gardens I sat on an iron chair in the sun, the metal hurting my bottom through my muslin dress. After a while I spread my legs and keep the material taut, I am wearing nothing underneath and people can see my sex. A group of men go jogging by, I beckon to one and take him behind a clump of foliage.

September 30

This cannot go on much longer, I have few illusions left, I am willing to have any man, any phallus, a woman. My head is whirling, I have sunk low, anything is good for an orgasm. I am a wild animal permanently on heat, I have lost all sense of control. I shall be picked up by the police soon, I can see it coming.

October 2

Thank God, I have found my analyst.

We exchanged a look, shook hands and within minutes I knew this was the one. I did not even harbour any sexual designs on him.

He is oldish, of sturdy build, slow in movement, and the reliable type. I trust his limpid blue eyes, he is attentive, I know he is going to understand.

He is not icy, tense, stuffy or play-acting like the others. We sat in armchairs and chatted away. I told him how I wanted sex all the time, how I kept swinging between elation and gloom, how I was full of contradictions, how confused I was.

'Do you think I can possibly pull out of this?'

He could have been evasive, replying 'What do you think?' or not even bothering to answer.

All he said was: 'Yes.'

It seems absurd but that little word filled me with happiness. I threw myself onto his lap and gave him a great big kiss on the cheek. He showed no surprise but took it naturally. He is my real daddy.

October 5

Today I went on the couch for the first time.

It is a leather couch, low in height, with a rust-coloured piece of material on it. There were two pillows, one on the other, and a small carpet thing for the feet, in case it was a rainy day!

In accordance with Freud's method, I could not see the analyst and faced away from him, but he could watch me.

At first I was uneasy: 'This is not very convenient for speaking.'

'Why's that?'

'You are sitting and I am lying down.'

'That's the usual way it's done.'

'But why must I lie down? I could sit too, or stand up even.'

'People think in a different way when they lie down.'

'How do they think then?'

'That's not for me to say, you'll see how you get along. You can always get up if you really want to.'

'No, let's keep it orthodox. So fire away, I am lying down. Where do we start?' Silence. 'What do we start with, what shall I tell you?' No comment. 'The first thing I remember, my childhood, my first disappointment, what do you want to know? Please tell me, what should I say?'

He speaks: 'There is no must about it, you know. You are

153

not being interrogated. Say whatever occurs to you, without sorting it out, let it come on its own.'

'That's not going to be easy, my ideas are often all mixed up, they come in waves simultaneously. Take that painting over there, when I look at it I think of several things at once...'

'Tell me one of them.'

'Well, a horse. I don't know what the painting's supposed to be, but it makes me think of a horse...'

I stop, aware that he is almost touching me, waiting and listening. I think of horses in the Camargue country in Provence, a white stallion with an erection, with a fantastically long member. I don't talk, I let the pictures go through my mind.

My analyst interrupts with a quiet 'Yes?' and I realize I ought to say something: 'I was thinking of horses, in the Camargue, about a horse I saw as a little girl. The stallion was on his back legs and he put his tummy against the mare and I was fascinated by his thing, his big organ, and I felt funny. I think I must have dreamed that...'

October 8

The analyst has fixed up two appointments a week, and I asked him how long the sessions would probably go on for.

'Two years, perhaps 10, perhaps longer.'

'I can't believe it, I couldn't possibly carry on for 10 whole years, or even eight or four.'

'That is very positive of you, wanting to move ahead quickly.'

'Let's say two years, three at the most. How does that look to you?'

'Just fine.' I want to cry on his shoulder in gratitude.

I feel exalted, a great adventure is beginning, I shall attempt to become the person I really am, the person I don't know yet. Obstacles will be swept away, pretences thrown aside, I shall be getting closer week by week to reality.

I can honestly say that today I began a new existence. I am not sorry about the eventful past months, no doubt I had to go through that. No doubt too I shall see things in better perspective as a result of the analysis.

I am entering this new life such a happy person. I am so full of joy at the prospect. Everything's going to be alright.

October 10
On the couch: 'I had better start with the day Osvaldo and I were sitting at the *terrace* at *Fouquet's*. We had arranged to meet Jemal there and suddenly I saw him coming up Avenue George V...'

STAR BOOKS ADULT READS

FICTION

BEATRICE	*Anonymous*	£2.25*
EVELINE	*Anonymous*	£1.95*
MORE EVELINE	*Anonymous*	£1.95*
FRANK AND I	*Anonymous*	£1.95
A MAN WITH A MAID	*Anonymous*	£2.25*
A MAN WITH A MAID II	*Anonymous*	£1.95*
A MAN WITH A MAID III	*Anonymous*	£1.95*
OH WICKED COUNTRY!	*Anonymous*	£1.95
ROMANCE OF LUST VOL I	*Anonymous*	£2.25*
ROMANCE OF LUST VOL II	*Anonymous*	£2.25*
SUBURBAN SOULS VOL I	*Anonymous*	£1.95*
SUBURBAN SOULS VOL II	*Anonymous*	£1.95*
DELTA OF VENUS	*Anaïs Nin*	£1.60*
LITTLE BIRDS	*Anaïs Nin*	£1.60*
PLAISIR D'AMOUR	*Anne-Marie Villefranche*	£2.25
JOIE D'AMOUR	*Anne-Marie Villefranche*	£1.95

STAR Books are obtainable from many booksellers and newsagents. If you have any difficulty tick the titles you want and fill in the form below.

Name _____

Address _____

_____

Send to: Star Books Cash Sales, P.O. Box 11, Falmouth, Cornwall, TR10 9EN.

Please send a cheque or postal order to the value of the cover price plus:
UK: 55p for the first book, 22p for the second book and 14p for each additional book ordered to the maximum charge of £1.75.

BFPO and EIRE: 55p for the first book, 22p for the second book, 14p per copy for the next 7 books, thereafter 8p per book.

OVERSEAS: £1.00 for the first book and 25p per copy for each additional book.

While every effort is made to keep prices low, it is sometimes necessary to increase prices at short notice. Star Books reserve the right to show new retail prices on covers which may differ from those advertised in the text or elsewhere.

NOT FOR SALE IN CANADA

STAR BOOKS ADULT READS

FICTION

THE ADVENTURES OF A SCHOOLBOY	*Anonymous*	£2.25
THE AUTOBIOGRAPHY OF A FLEA	*Anonymous*	£2.25*
ALTAR OF VENUS	*Anonymous*	£2.25*
MEMOIRES OF DOLLY MORTON	*Anonymous*	£1.95
LAURA MIDDLETON	*Anonymous*	£1.95
THREE TIMES A WOMAN	*Anonymous*	£2.25*
THE BOUDOIR	*Anonymous*	£2.25*
THE LUSTFUL TURK	*Anonymous*	£2.25*
MAUDIE	*Anonymous*	£2.25
RANDIANA	*Anonymous*	£2.25*
ROSA FIELDING	*Anonymous*	£2.25*
JOY	*Joy Laurey*	£1.95
JOY AND JOAN	*Joy Laurey*	£2.25
OPUS PISTORUM	*Henry Miller*	£2.25*
INSTRUMENT OF PLEASURE	*Celeste Piano*	£2.25

STAR Books are obtainable from many booksellers and newsagents. If you have any difficulty tick the titles you want and fill in the form below.

Name _____

Address _____

_____

Send to: Star Books Cash Sales, P.O. Box 11, Falmouth, Cornwall, TR10 9EN.

Please send a cheque or postal order to the value of the cover price plus:
 UK: 55p for the first book, 22p for the second book and 14p for each additional book ordered to the maximum charge of £1.75.

BFPO and EIRE: 55p for the first book, 22p for the second book, 14p per copy for the next 7 books, thereafter 8p per book.

OVERSEAS: £1.00 for the first book and 25p per copy for each additional book.

While every effort is made to keep prices low, it is sometimes necessary to increase prices at short notice. Star Books reserve the right to show new retail prices on covers which may differ from those advertised in the text or elsewhere.

NOT FOR SALE IN CANADA